A Swim Back Home

by

Denise Sawyer

Romagnoli Publications

This book was printed in the
United States of America.

First Edition

ISBN-13: 978-1-891486-16-6

Romagnoli Publications

email: romagnoli.publications@gmail.com
website: www.romagnoli-publications.com

Reviews

A Swim Back Home is a poignant tale of longing for childhood and the wish to return and change that one thing that would make everything right. When that chance seems to be handed to Renee, she is forced to weigh the possible costs to her family - a process that changes her as much as any tinkering of the past would do. With humor and wisdom, Sawyer expertly interweaves the conflicts between adult reality and childhood yearnings, and between fantasy and reality, into a compelling tapestry that is a joy to read.
Edward H. Jacobs, Ph.D.— author of *Fathering the ADHD Child* and *ADHD: Helping Parents Help Their Children*

Dedication

This book is dedicated to the members of my writing group: Linda, Ed, and Josh. Without your encouragement and excellent feedback, *A Swim Back Home* would have been recycled into paper straws. I thank you guys from the bottom of my heart. As Linda liked to say, "I love us."

Denise Sawyer

In childhood, we press our nose to the pane, looking out. In memories of childhood, we press our nose to the pane, looking in.   **Robert Brault**

Denise Sawyer

CHAPTER ONE

I wasn't planning on going in the pool that day. The sky threatened rain and it was on the cool side, but my husband and I were having our usual tired argument about my collecting things, and then John goes and drops his little nugget: "So when were you going to tell me about the storage unit, Renee?"

I was thinking NEVER, John, but I couldn't tell him that. It's not like I'm a hoarder; I just like collecting mementos from the 1960s, specifically *Life* magazines, newspapers, albums, posters, and yes, I admit, some furniture. If I were a hoarder though, I would have piles of garbage reaching to the ceiling. The *Life* magazines are stacked neatly under the living room couch. You can hardly see them. So I wondered how he found out about the storage unit. Now that I was retired, I always brought in the mail.

Although I had woken up with a terrible headache that morning, he had kindly waited until the four Tylenol had numbed my headache to spar with me. He stood at the foot of the bed and tossed the Pack-A-Way Self Storage bill in my lap. Attached to the late notice was a sticky note written in the formal cursive hand of our neighbor next door. Her note said she found the bill mixed in with her mail and that she was sorry it took so long to get it to us. I reached over to John's nightstand and took a sip of his coffee. It was black and bitter. "So, did you go there?"

"Yeah, Renee, I found the key," he said solemnly. "First you turn every room into a Mid Century throwback, and then I find a storage unit full of even more crap." He headed for the master bath.

"You didn't seem to mind hauling my father's old workbench all the way up from Massachusetts," I said dumbly.

John abruptly turned around. "That was five years ago. I knew how much that monstrosity meant to you and besides, nobody else in your family would take it."

When I didn't respond, he went into the bathroom and started brushing shaving cream on his face from a bar of shaving soap he kept in a metal dish by the sink.

"John, it's my money," I said, watching his reflection shave in the bathroom mirror.

He put down the razor and stood in the doorway. "You're the one who wants to sell the house and buy a condo in Florida. Where were you going to park the workbench, huh, Renee?" He turned back to the mirror. "This is crazy," he said to his reflection. Then he shut the door.

John didn't understand what it was like to move several states away from your friends and relatives right before entering the sixth grade. My parents robbed me of the life I was supposed to have in New Jersey. John would never get it because he never left New Hampshire. I waited until I heard the shower running before I threw off the covers in disgust. "I'm going for a swim," I mumbled to the bathroom door.

* * *

A low mist had covered the slick lawn. I opened and re-latched the pool gate quietly. It was still early, but I didn't want to alert the widower next door. He had a wildlife camera supposedly fixed on his backyard, but lately he had been making skinny-dipping innuendos.

The early morning headache started to make a comeback, but I ignored it. Diving had always calmed me. And I wanted to practice a few dives before John went to work, not that I was any good. He didn't like me diving when no one was home saying, "What if you crack your head on the bottom?"

I watched the robotic pool vacuum we called Rosie zip around in the deep end. John had thrown her in the night before. He had set her up on a cleaning schedule with a timer to clean every night. My job was to toss her in after I was done swimming for the day, but I kept forgetting. I was also forgetting to close the garage doors and the porch slider. John gave up and silently threw Rosie in the pool each night before securing the house. I looked at the timer. She had another fifteen minutes of cleaning left. I considered taking her out; however, she was heavy. I decided to leave her in. I'd swim around her. Down at the deep end, her power supply sat safely on the pool deck, plugged into an electrical outlet in the pool house. Although a little frayed, her long blue cord was plugged into the other end of the power supply. I waded in up to my waist. The water was refreshingly cool. I plunged under the water, hoping that the shock of cold water on my head would freeze out the headache.

The sun peeked through a hole in the thick cloud cover, and I dreamily watched the sun cast shimmering aqua-colored ripples on the bottom of the pool. The ripples formed an iridescent chain link fence that do-si-doed around itself, collapsing and reforming new links.

I surfaced and smoothed back my hair. My mind drifted back to John. Yes, the workbench was a heavy wooden hulk as tall as an altar. It took up the entire back wall of the garage. Back in the 1950s, it was my father's old drafting desk. He had carted it home from the plant after they gave him a newer, snazzier desk. With its deep wooden drawers and center cabinet, it made an excellent workbench. For sixty years, it stood silently in garages, first in Colonia, New Jersey, then in Massachusetts, and finally up here in New Hampshire. Each smear of paint was a tiny snapshot in time, proof of ordinary lives lived.

I could never part with this family heirloom. They have self-storage units in Florida too. I bet there are LOTS of storage units down there. People were retiring and hauling stuff from their hometowns where they had lived all their lives.

The last time I saw my childhood home was maybe 20 years ago. I received a fancy invitation to my Uncle Gene's 80th birthday party. I was brimming with anticipation when I backed out of my driveway in New Hampshire for the five-hour drive down to the mecca of my childhood. During the party, my cousins and I reminisced about Christmases spent together, like the Christmas when my cousin Stephen played scary music on an old piano in his cellar and then ran up the stairs and locked the door. After the party, I was riding in my cousin Anne's car when the four-glasses-of-wine melancholy set in. As we drove along the Garden State Parkway, I told Anne how lucky she was to have lived her whole life in one town and then inherited her parents' house.

"Yeah, but the neighborhood is shot to hell, Renee, and I can't afford to live anywhere else," she said, weaving around a slow-moving pickup truck.

"But you could have lunch with someone you went to kindergarten with," I remember telling her.

"Yeah, but I don't. Besides, everyone moved away as soon as they could."

I told her that I would have stuck around and that I was devastated when we moved to Massachusetts for my father's new job back in 1966. That's when Anne suggested we drive by the house.

As much as I longed to see my cherished childhood home, I wasn't sure I could handle any snooty upgrades or homesteads ravaged by time. It was meant to be flash-frozen like a yearbook photo of the high school hunk. You don't want that memory tapping you on the shoulder at Trader Joe's to look like Homer Simpson. But I yearned to see my home again. My heart quickened as Anne merged smoothly onto a busy street lined with strip malls. Although the street had a vaguely familiar- sounding name, nothing looked familiar. However, when we rounded the corner onto Lake Avenue, I held my breath, waiting for Lake's candy store to appear on the next corner. "PULL IN HERE!" I shouted.

Lake's wasn't there. In its place was a bank, hogging most of the plaza. Also crammed in there was a pizza place, a dry cleaner, and a salon, all with garish neon signage on their large glass front windows. "What the hell!"

Anne turned off the engine. "Were you expecting it to look the same?"

The wine buzz had worn off, and now I was irritated. "Yes, I expected the old clapboard store with its creaky wooden floor, and huge candy counter to be right where I left it." I took a breath. "Let's go around the corner and see what the rest of the block looks like," I told her.

When we turned onto Cameo Place, the neighborhood redeemed itself. I was pleased to see that the original 1950's look-alike split levels had survived. However, as we drove further into the development, many of the starter homes were replaced by showy 4-bedroom colonials wedged into their quarter-acre lots. As if to prove their superiority, their taller silhouettes cast menacing shadows over the older homes.

"I think you went past my house, Anne."

The GPS agreed and ordered her to turn around. Rolling slowly back up the street, Anne came to a stop in front of a hulking, dirty green dumpster parked in a crumbling driveway. Tall pieces of rotting lumber stuck out of the dumpster. They looked like wooden swords abandoned after a noble fight. Where my house was supposed to be, was a deep pit blocked off by a wobbly, orange construction fence.

"They tore down my house!" I hollered out the window. Then I undid my seatbelt and got out of the car.

"Where are you going?" Anne said from behind the wheel.

I strode up the driveway. When I reached the dumpster, I hefted myself up and peered over the edge, catching a whiff of rotting wood and age. I was hoping there would be something I could salvage. I was mildly aware of what a nut job I must have looked like to neighbors peeking through kitchen windows. Shoving over pieces of fake stone siding, I searched for something familiar: the pink tile from the upstairs bathroom or perhaps the laundry room cabinets my father had built. Nothing.

Feeling defeated, I jumped down from the dumpster and walked towards the pit. Next to the deep hole, lying on its side like a fallen horse, was the old weeping willow tree, root ball exposed. Something glinted under the tangle of snake-like roots. That's when I found Audrey's Magic 8-Ball.

"What are you doing?"

I snapped my head around to see Anne standing over me with her hands on her hips. "Look what I found," I had said, handing her the ball.

She wiped off the dirt and turned it over. "It's one of those Magic 8-Balls, and it's a really old one. See, it's made of glass, not plastic." She held it out and pointed to the faded number 8 printed on the top side of the ball.

When I turned it over, we saw cloudy, gray liquid floating under a small triangle of cracked glass.

"Why was it buried?" Anne asked.

"Who knows, but it's the last memento I'll ever have from my home. And besides, it'll just end up in that dumpster. I'll polish it up and use it as a paperweight or something." I stroked it like a cat. "Hey, Magic 8-Ball, aren't you glad I dug you up?" After I gave it a good long shake, I turned it over. Anne moved in closer, and we waited for the broken toy to awaken from its long sleep. The 8-Ball never did wake up, but I still took it home and stuffed it in the storage unit.

* * *

The headache and wooziness dissipated, so I maneuvered around Rosie's long cord and made my way to the diving board. When I hoisted myself out of the pool, I thought about taking Rosie out again, but I didn't. She had scooted down to the shallow end anyway and was busy rolling up and down the walls of the pool. As I trotted down the diving board, I heard John on the porch opening the slider. Damn, is it that time already? I bounced hard at the end of the board and hurled myself up high enough to attempt a jackknife. I angled my torso down, touched the arches of my feet, and then straightened myself out to hopefully finish with a headfirst dive. I didn't quite nail it. Instead of my head piercing the water, it was my chest. It created an explosive splash, and it hurt.

Down at the shallow end, the force of my clumsy dive sent Rosie crashing upside down against the ladder at the 3-foot depth. After a pause, she righted herself and slipped under the water like an alligator. Rather than completing her housekeeping in the shallows, she changed course and charged at me in a flurry of indignant bubbles. As I broke the surface of the water, she sideswiped me, then ensnared my legs in her long cord. I started to sink. Where was John? He should have been down here by now. Rosie sent up a few warning bubbles before plunging to the bottom of the deep end. I felt myself sinking, slowly at first, then more insistently aided by a steady downward suction. The funny thing was, I didn't feel panicky. It was more like a dreamy weightlessness as if I were a dry leaf drifting along on a gentle autumn breeze. When my body touched the bottom, I felt a tug at my ankle. From the corner of my eye, I saw a figure of a little girl in white pajamas. Her long floating hair obscured her pale face. She was reaching out from inside the pool drain. I needed to breathe. I snapped out of my trance-like stupor and tried to shake her off, but she held on firmly. Then she pulled me down the drain.

In a moment, we were both submerged in a small white chamber. I popped up and gasped for air. High above me, I could see the drain grate. If I could just punch it open, I could free myself from this watery chamber. I propelled myself upwards, but just before I reached it, a strong current sucked me back underwater and into the chamber. My lungs filled with water. The thought that I didn't want to think settled over me; I was drowning, and this was the in-between place where life meets death, yet I felt untroubled, no longer feeling the need to breathe.

Ahead, I could see that the chamber opened into a narrow blue tunnel. The girl in the pajamas let go of my ankle and glided towards the tunnel, motioning over her shoulder for me to follow.

I didn't want to.

She turned around and hovered close to my face. Her dazzling hazel eyes soon mesmerized me into calmness. I bobbed along behind her, riding a lazy river deep into the tunnel.

The water was warmer in here. We came to a bend and in the distance, I spotted what looked like the end of the tunnel. She waited for me there. When I reached it, I saw that the tunnel ended at a jellyfish-like membrane. The tranquility I had been feeling earlier started to wear off.

With her palm, she pressed against the center of the membrane. It opened slightly and through it, I caught a glimpse of blue skies. And clouds? I was both comforted and terrified by this image. Where was she taking me? She motioned for me to go through, but I wanted her to go first. Perhaps I could escape back through the tunnel.

She started to fidget a bit, twisting her body back and forth, and that's when I noticed that the tunnel was growing darker and the water had cooled. She kept her eyes focused on the tunnel as if watching for someone or some thing. She turned back to me with a pleading look, urgently motioning me to go through the membrane.

It started as a low rumbling sound. As it grew louder, the tunnel walls started collapsing around us. There was only one way out. I dove through the center of the membrane.

CHAPTER TWO

The membrane was slimy. Passing through it, the girl in the pajamas sideswiped me as she dashed ahead of me. When the membrane spit me out, I felt myself sinking to the bottom of a tank of water. It was cold, colder than the tunnel water, much colder. There was movement in the tank too. I opened my eyes. My sight was blurry, but I could make out little legs and feet, pairs of them, all around me, some bouncing up and down on one foot. I searched for the girl in the pajamas among the sea of legs and feet, but she had abandoned me. Annoyed as I was, there was a growing tightness in my chest; I needed to breathe. I swam upward and broke the surface of the water. Under a blinding sun, I inhaled a full, glorious lungful of air and then another.

Wait. Wasn't I dead?

A preteen boy was perched at the top of an aluminum pool ladder. Water dripped from the hem of his maroon bathing suit. He shook out his skinny freckled arms and poised himself for a launch into the pool.

"Hey, you," I called to him, startled by the sound of my child-like voice that I did not recognize. Clearing my throat, I called louder. My voice was the same. Stay calm, I told myself. The boy fixed his eyes on me. My vision hadn't cleared completely, but I knew who he was: my brother. "Kiel?"

"What?"

"Kiel, am I dead?"

"No, but I wish you were. Get out of the way!" And with that, he gathered up his legs like a praying mantis and cannonballed into the pool. I was too stunned to move. If I weren't dead, was I in some sort of way station with my brother who also wasn't dead? As I let out a scream, Kiel crash-landed on my head. The blow knocked me under in a wave of fizzy bubbles. And then everything clicked off.

* * *

I woke up in a green hammock. A feeling of dread, like the kind you feel after a stressful dream that you can't quite remember, seeped into me. My forehead throbbed, and there was something cold perched on top of my head. I reached up and pulled off a green ice bag that looked like a giant beanbag. Under the cold spot, I felt a small lump above my right eye. There was also a tingling under my right ear.

I swung my legs down and sat up, gripping the hem of the hammock as it lurched back and forth. The sky had clouded over. A few drops of rain speckled my face, first tentatively then more insistently. A woman's voice called out to me. "Get in the house, Renee. There's a thunderstorm coming." The sky agreed, punctuating her sentence with a righteous rumble of thunder.

I focused hard on the woman calling from a side door. Her blonde hair was done up in a 60's style flip. She waited in the shadows, holding the screen door open for me. "HOW'S YOUR HEAD?" she shouted across the yard.

Mom?

I wanted to scream with joy and tell her how thrilled I was to see her and ask her why she was here with me now and a million other things. Still, I just sat there shivering, unable to speak, unable to comprehend what my mind was broadcasting: the white clapboard house with red shutters and red trim was my early childhood home in New Jersey. Does this mean that I am dead? Dead like my mother?

Through a curtain of rain, I staggered across the yard past a redwood picnic table littered with lopsided Dixie cups.

"You better get out of that damp suit," my mother warned as I stumbled up the steps.

* * *

And there I was, back in the Colonia, New Jersey kitchen in some snapshot of time. The stove was there on the right and the narrow Formica peninsula on the left. It smelled the same as I remembered. I scanned the top of the fridge and found the green bottle of Airwick Air Freshener with its thick tongue-like wick protruding from the top.

I gave my mother a big hug. She smelled of cigarettes and hairspray. "I'm feeling a little foggy-headed," I stammered. Over her shoulder, I searched for a calendar that was usually tacked up near the peninsula. There was none. Christ, what year is this? In the calmest voice I could muster I said, "I'll go change."

Up ahead was the living room and a set of stairs that led down to my favorite room, the rec room. I wanted to go down there and explore the fluorescent-lit room with its black and white checkered linoleum that was good for sliding around in socks and weaving bikes around the poles. I wondered if anyone was sitting in one of the blue vinyl chairs that regularly got knocked backward with one of us kids holding on for dear life. I lingered at the top of the rec room stairs and listened. I could hear the old black and white TV talking earnestly.

Next to the rec room stairs was another set of stairs leading up to the second floor. I reached for the wrought iron railing and headed upstairs, peeking in doorways as I made my way down the hall to the pink and black tiled bathroom. No one was up here. I was grateful for the solitude. The throbbing on my forehead intensified. I needed Tylenol, and I needed to calm myself down.

The thunderstorm, still raging outside, kept the bathroom mercifully dark. With my heart fluttering, I shut the door behind me, careful not to glance in the mirror just yet. I didn't want to face what I already knew. After taking a couple of deep breaths, I steadied myself in front of the mirror and slowly raised my head.

A silhouette of a petite girl with a disheveled pixie stared back at me. I flicked on the light switch. The face was pale with a spray of freckles across the nose and cheeks. But it was the fearful eyes peering back at me that triggered a flush of cold sweat to sweep up my back. I cupped a hand over my mouth, stifling a gasp. How could this be? On the outside, I was a child indeed, but on the inside, I held all the memories and regrets of my sixty-seven years. Why? A wave of churning nausea prickled my stomach and then percolated up to my throat. I dashed over to the pink toilet and yanked up the seat. Waves of dry heaves convulsed through me. When it was over, I laid down on the blessedly cold tile floor.

I stayed on the floor for several minutes. I didn't want to move, but sooner or later, my mother would come looking for me. I pulled myself up and washed and dried my face at the sink. Then I opened the aluminum medicine cabinet behind the mirror. Inside was a box of Alka-Seltzer, a tube of Ben- Gay and a bottle of Bufferin. The Bufferin would do, I thought, tapping out two tablets in my palm. When I put the Bufferin back, I noticed a prescription bottle from Dell's Pharmacy on the top shelf. I had to stand on my tippy toes to reach it. The label read *Librium 10 mg. Take one every four hours* as needed. It was for my mother, and the bottle was full. My mother took tranquilizers? I put the bottle back with the label facing out, just like it was.

At the other end of the hall had to be the bedroom I shared with my younger sister Audrey. I closed the medicine cabinet and headed down there. The room was large with light pink painted walls. Two welcoming twin beds, parallel to each other with a nightstand between them, stood out from one wall. The twin bed nestled in the corner was piled high with naked dolls. On the other side of the room was my white desk and chair, embellished with gold paint in the grooves, the same desk that sat in my spare bedroom up in New Hampshire—in the future.

This bedroom was my refuge from the unfairness of life, like the time my Uncle Gene got tickets to see the Beatles at Shea Stadium but only for the teenage cousins.

Tacked up on the wall above the desk was a calendar opened to a photo of a waving American flag. The calendar said it was July 1966. That meant I was 11. Christ, what an awkward age. Why couldn't I have come back as a teen? I was robbed of those years watching the neighborhood boys grow into handsome teenagers, flirting with them, and then graduating from Colonia High School with all my friends. I wondered how long I was supposed to be here, wherever here was: days, months, forever? If it was an extended stay, I guess I'd get my redo. But then there would be no John. He put up with me for thirty-five years. Would he miss me? Probably not. He was fed up with my collecting. He's probably thinking "good riddance". My stomach made an uncomfortable rumble. Stay calm.

I looked around the cheerful bedroom. Next to the desk was a big white bureau. I pulled out a few heavy drawers stuffed with clothes in tangled heaps. I pulled out a pair of wrinkled shorts that looked familiar. My mother had sewn Audrey and me tops and shorts from black and white striped fabric with watermelons that looked suspiciously like tablecloth material. I hated the outfit. I rummaged around some more and found another shorts set that looked my size. Still, it was a shock when I stepped out of my bathing suit and saw a flat chest, narrow hips, and no hair down below. I sat on the edge of the bed and got dressed, taking in my new/old surroundings. Although I could have used a few more years of retirement, this is your new home now, the Heaven you always wanted.

* * *

Outside the rain had stopped, leaving a steamy haze over Westminster Road. Water flowed down gutter grates, making hollow gushing sounds. There was another sound. Someone was coming upstairs.

"ARE YOU OKAY NOW?"

Oh My God. It was my eight-year-old sister, Audrey. Because she was hard of hearing, Audrey only spoke at one volume— loud. "I've been better."

"WHAT?"

"I'm FINE," I shouted back at her.

Audrey stared at me for a moment and then plopped on the twin bed in the corner. She dug out a hard black ball from under her pillow.

"AM I GOING TO GROW UP AND MARRY GEORGE HARRISON?" Audrey asked.

When she shook the ball and turned it over, I realized it was one of those Magic 8-Balls that everyone wanted one Christmas. Audrey frowned. "IT SAYS TO ASK AGAIN LATER."

Wait. Was this the same Magic 8-Ball I had dug up from the property years ago? No. That would be too weird. I started to feel light-headed again. Just breathe, Renee.

"EARTH TO RENEE! DO YOU WANT A TURN?"

Audrey's shouting jolted me out of my thoughts. "Nah." But curiosity got the better of me. I waited until Audrey stashed the 8-Ball back under her pillow and went downstairs before retrieving it, mindful of how crazy it was to seek counsel from a toy. So was crash-landing in your personal Never Neverland. I asked, "Am I supposed to be here?" I gave it a good shake, turned it over, and waited for words to float under its glass-bottom-boat belly.

Outlook good.

I stared at the words for a long time, unable to accept that this toy confirmed my existence here.

I swallowed my fear and asked THE question; "Am I dead?" Then I gave the 8-Ball a good cocktail shaker shake and rolled it over on the bed.

Better not tell you now.

In a way, I was comforted by the response. Perhaps this place was just a stopover on the way to my final resting place: death. I should savor my layover until the end, so I asked the 8-Ball if I would be here long.

The cloudy liquid sloshed teasingly under the glass for several seconds. Then the Magic 8-Ball blinked a tiny, lightning-bug pulse of light and streamed:

Better not tell you now.
Better not tell you now.
Better not tell you now.

CHAPTER THREE

I didn't remember going to sleep or even waking up, but there I was, sitting at the kitchen table with a pounding headache on that first morning of being dead, resurrected, or whatever. Kiel was practicing a card trick. Audrey was walking a Midge doll, now appropriately dressed, across the table. My mother seemed unusually quiet, not telling them to "get that stuff off the table."

My mother placed a bottle of orange juice on the table. I had forgotten about that glass bottle. For decades she would mix up a can of store-brand orange juice concentrate and put it in this old tomato juice bottle. She was still doing it in her 80s when fresh orange juice came in cartons, and my parents' retirement kitty was plentiful.

I snapped out of my old life daydream when the toaster popped up two half-charred waffles. My mother gingerly pinched them out and added them to Audrey's plate.

Audrey thanked her in Pig Latin, "ANKS-THAY." Then she hefted the bottle of Log Cabin syrup with both hands and poured an amber pool over her waffles.

"Audrey, no Pig Latin at the table," my mother said in an irritable, sing-song voice that made Kiel snicker at Audrey. My mother cleared her throat. "Kids, listen. Dad's expecting a very important letter. I'm going to the beauty parlor so whoever brings in the mail, make sure it ends up on the counter."

"What's the letter for?" Kiel asked, not looking up as he sliced through his pallet of syrupy waffles.

My mother poured herself a cup of coffee and leaned against the stove. "Well, you know we talked about Dad looking for a new job. He's waiting to hear from a plant that builds missiles."

Kiel stopped chewing, "Cool. Where?"

She sat at the table and reached for the crinkled pack of Pall Malls next to her. We waited while she shook out a cigarette. "Massachusetts."

The fork slipped out of my hand and clattered against the plate. In a clear neon-flashing revelation, I realized that this was the moment 56 years ago that set me off course. First, you're riding in a shiny red wagon filled with friends and cousins and safe adventures. You're pulled along by grown-ups, school, and the seasons where rhythms are set for you. Sundays and holidays were full of aunts and uncles speaking Italian at long tables. And then the heartbreak of moving day tosses you right out of that wagon. You tearfully hug goodbye to friends you'll never see again while you watch sweaty movers heft your bed into a dirty Mayflower moving van. Once you land in Massachusetts, you struggle to find your footing in the loneliness of a grammar school built in 1895 filled with the unfriendly glances of giggling girls. In high school, another old building, you make yourself invisible because you're too pimply, too skinny, and too self-conscious to ever be cool.

"But I don't want to move," Kiel croaked.

In defiance of the breakfast table executive order, Audrey shouted in Pig Latin her displeasure as well. My mother let this slide. She flicked the lighter and lit her cigarette. We watched her take a long, angry drag from her tangerine-painted lips and point a plume of smoke toward the light fixture.

"First of all, nothing may come of it. Second, we can't live in this house forever; it's too small for the five of us, so you kids better get used to the idea." With that, she stubbed out her cigarette and got up from the table. "Just watch for the postman, alright?"

* * *

After breakfast, I stood at the kitchen window and watched my mother back down the driveway in her light blue Volkswagen bug. My mother never wanted to move. This I knew. Her ten siblings and mother lived here. My father's family lived eight hours away in Maine. For decades after moving to Massachusetts, my mother constantly compared her beloved New Jersey to New England describing New Englanders as cold.

The postman never came before lunch; that I remembered, so I had time to, to do what? Swipe the letter? Would Raytheon then assume my father no longer wanted the job? Maybe. And if I was truly dead or close to it, this is where I wanted to be.

Breakfast did nothing to curb my headache, so I headed to the bathroom for more Bufferin. When I reached into the medicine cabinet, I noticed that the

Librium bottle had been moved. My mother seemed a little brighter before she left, and I wondered if she popped one before getting behind the wheel in that tin can with no seatbelts. I opened the lid and counted the pills. Twenty-eight left. I thought about taking a Librium myself. However, I would need all my wits to cope with whatever lay ahead. I settled for the Bufferin.

Before the aspirin kicked in, I stepped out into the summer morning sunshine. Being back in ankle socks and my cherished white Keds soothed me. The sneakers were smudged around the toes, but I resisted the urge to clean them. You're supposed to be 11 now, not 67. My mother would be gone for hours, plenty of time for me to do some exploring and still be back before the postman came. I stared down Westminster Road, mesmerized by the pristine state of the homes. The headache dissipated, and a joyful calmness spread over me. "You're home now, Renee," I whispered to myself as I crossed to the other side of Westminster Road. Then I headed for my beloved elementary school, School 17.

* * *

As I walked along the sidewalk, I window-shopped every property I passed. Colorful flower boxes hung under kitchen windows. Bikes and scooters sunned themselves in driveways, and an occasional Our Lady of the Bathtub shrine watched over families from front lawns. The homes still had their one-car garages and no top-heavy additions to desecrate them. So far, this place was right out of my favorite recurring dream. So am I dead? I pondered that question as I walked toward the township's schools.

By the time I rounded the corner onto Caroline Place, the headache was just a nuzzle on my forehead. And there I was, standing in front of Colonia Jr. High. As a real kid, this imposing two-story red brick building was a mysterious place where teachers seemed to be recruited from a Charles Dickens novel, and the students sat at desks, stiff as statues. I grinned and continued down the sidewalk to School 17. I'd find the auditorium where we sang in concerts and performed in plays. The most memorable show was the famous Soupy Sales skit performed by my brother's class. The older kids had started a rumor that the comedian himself would make an appearance. I remember watching the auditorium's large double doors, waiting for Soupy Sales to burst in and take over the show. I was devastated when he didn't.

When I reached the parking lot of School 17, I noticed there were several cars parked there. I didn't expect to see so many because it was July. Stepping off the curb, I strolled through the lot, checking out the Ford Fairlanes, Falcons, Mustangs, and Volkswagen Beetles. The windows were rolled down on a blue Falcon. I stuck my head in. The steering wheel was skinny and very large, like a bicycle wheel. On the bench seat was a *Life* magazine. I read the date: July 1966. A black and white image of the moon's surface was on the cover. For a crazy moment, my thoughts returned to the *Life* magazine collection under my couch. Did I have this issue? Snap out of it, I told myself. You're living *Life* magazine right now. There was a low rumbling sound in the distance. I pulled my head out of the Falcon and started walking. The sound became increasingly louder and now seemed to be coming from behind me as if following me. I looked over my shoulder. A white Lincoln Navigator sped past me. Wait. What? This is supposed to be 1966. Why would a Twenty-first-century car be here? What the hell? The Navigator exited the parking lot and was gone. My heart began to race. Just calm down. There must be an explanation.

When I got back up on the sidewalk, I tried to block out what I had just seen and let School 17's welcoming one-story red brick building calm me. Several kid-height narrow windows running across the front of the school were open. Good. That meant the school was open, and I could get inside and explore. There was a clang. School 17's double doors opened. Two women, deep in conversation, strolled out. One was wearing pink pedal pushers, and the other a floral sleeveless shift. I let out my breath. Order was restored. When they passed me on the sidewalk, they gave me that condescending smile adults pull out just for kids. When I reached for the door handle, I heard a familiar pesky chime. I whirled around to see Pedal Pusher reach into her pocket and pull out a cell phone. No, this was all wrong. I waited for her to lift the phone to her ear. She didn't. Instead, she offered the phone to her friend. But when her friend reached for it, the phone recomposed itself into a pack of cigarettes.

I bolted, running behind the school, across the playground, and down to the parking lot of St. John Vianney Church. And then I kept running, reaching the woods, panting and sweating. When I got to a clearing, I knelt in the shady coolness of damp brush and fanned the shirt away from my sweaty back. What was this strange land where time layered over itself like a double-exposed photo? "Will someone please tell me what the hell is going on?" I yelled up at the treetops.

I waited, but the trees didn't conveniently turn into cell phone towers, nor did the discarded cigarette packs lying about shape-shift into cell phones. Would I have tried to call John to come get me if they had? Not so fast, I realized with a stab of guilt. Being here was a gift, wasn't it? After my heart stopped pounding, I climbed the embankment to the Inman Avenue overpass. Maybe these hallucinations were just the last gasps of my life before. I tried to con myself into believing this.

Below, cars rushed by on the Garden State Parkway. I scanned the parkway for any more vehicles from Tomorrowland. There weren't any. This calmed me a bit, so I stepped onto the quiet overpass.

I was halfway over the bridge when I was abruptly pushed back by something. At first, I thought it was just an errant gust of wind that made me step backward, almost knocking me over. I stepped forward again. Held back again. It wasn't the wind. Reaching out, I felt something squishy and soft, like a beach ball. What the heck? I pressed again with both palms, and that's when I noticed a thin, translucent membrane in front of me. I looked high above and down by my feet. It was there too, walling me off like a force field.

A Rambler station wagon whizzed past me, and from the opposite direction, several cars and trucks made their way across the overpass. The force field hadn't stopped them. No, no no! I kicked at the membrane. It eased slightly initially, but with each subsequent kick, the membrane hardened as if to defend itself. I willed myself not to panic. Colonia High School, currently under construction, and of course, the rest of the civilized world was on the other side. If this were my forever home, I would need to figure out how to break through this barrier and soon. Defeated, I glanced up at the sun. It was approaching noon. My stomach grumbled in agreement. I needed to eat. I'd figure this out.

On the walk home, I kept my head down so I wouldn't see anything else morph into the next century's finest marvels. I thought about the Librium.

My mother had not gotten back from the beauty parlor. On the front lawn was a boy's bike laying on its side. Its chrome handlebars gleamed in the sun. It was still too early for the mailman, but I lifted the lid of the mailbox that hung next to the front door anyway. It was empty. Good. I still had time to snatch the Raytheon letter. I would help my father find another job right here in New Jersey. My mother would certainly appreciate that, and it would change the trajectory of all of our lives. Yeah, but is it right? I pushed down a tickle of guilt and then walked through the front door.

Audrey was sitting on the couch in the living room, sticking and unsticking Colorforms. She cocked her head as I headed upstairs. "WHERE'D YOU GO? I WAS ALL ALONE."

"WHERE'S KIEL? HE WAS HERE WHEN I LEFT," I shouted back.

"ALBERT CAME OVER, AND THEN THEY LEFT."

It took me a minute to remember who Albert was: Kiel's best friend and a hack magician. My brother was his sidekick. "Kiel shouldn't have left you by yourself. I have to go upstairs for a minute, but then I'll make you a fried Taylor Ham sandwich."

"YOU KNOW HOW TO COOK?"

Damn. "Just Taylor Ham and grilled cheese."

Audrey seemed satisfied and turned back to her Colorforms.

I headed upstairs to my bedroom. The Magic 8-Ball was still under Audrey's pillow. God, how does she sleep with that hard thing there? I held it in both hands like the head of a small child and spoke to it. "You need to cooperate and give me straight answers now. Alright? Am I dead?" I gave it a gentle shimmy.

I watched the gray liquid roll about before returning: **concentrate and ask again**.

I was in no mood for this passive-aggressive nonsense, but I complied and laid the 8-Ball on the bed for a moment to fake concentrate. When I picked up the ball again, it felt noticeably warmer. "Okay, let's back up a minute. Am I supposed to be here?" It was the same question I had asked when I arrived here. I gave it a quick side slosh.

As I see it, yes.

Two affirmative answers to the same question. Now we're getting somewhere. I snuck in something else I wondered about. "Who are you?" No response, just cloudy gray liquid. It took me a minute to realize that I had forgotten to ask in a yes/ no format, so I re-framed the question. "Are you my friend?"

Without a doubt.

For the next several minutes, I sat cross-legged on Audrey's bed and parleyed with the 8-Ball as it got warmer with each response. Yes, I could trust it.

Yes, the force field was real (and I should be wary). When the 8-Ball got so hot that I had to use Audrey's bedspread as a potholder, I circled back to THE burning question. "Am I dead?"

The cloudy gray liquid sloshed about teasingly for longer than it should have. When it was good and ready, it replied: **You may rely on it.**

Panic exploded in my chest, and my vision began to blur again. Just breathe. At least you know for sure now. I rested my head on Audrey's pillow until my vision cleared. I had one more question. I sat up and asked, "Is this Heaven?"

Through the bedspread potholder, I felt a slight wobbling, like a cell phone on vibrate. **Cannot predict now** floated up below the glass.

Tiny prickles of heat pinged my forehead, and then the headache resurfaced. I took a couple of deep breaths to steady myself. I asked the Heaven question several more times, but it seemed to be back on its auto-repeat loop of Cannot predict now. Giving up, I headed to the bathroom for more Bufferin.

I stared at the Librium bottle behind the Bufferin for a long time. So you're dead, Renee. Dead with headaches and hallucinations and an evasive 8-Ball. However, being back here is a gift, right? You'll get through this. Take a Librium. Before I could talk myself out of taking my mother's tranquilizer, I popped one in my mouth. It would help with the headache for sure. And with a little rest, I'd be able to cope with all that's been happening to me as well as figuring out how to get rid of that pesky force field.

Instead of going downstairs to make Audrey's sandwich and wait for the postman, I stretched out on my bed. The windows were open, and a gentle breeze puffed out the white eyelet curtains. So peaceful. I closed my eyes. Before long, I was wrapped in a pleasant embrace of a daydream of floating along in the water tunnel. I felt the presence of someone there with me, but I couldn't see them. Then the daydream was swept away. It didn't matter. I was adrift now, floating in a calming darkness.

Behind the darkness, I heard a faint voice. "Hang in there, Renee. Help is on the way." The voice was male, earnest and far away, too far away for me to care. I slept.

* * *

I opened my eyes a slit. Long afternoon shadows draped the bedroom walls, familiar walls. Audrey's pale, freckled face loomed over me. She gently shook my shoulder. "MOM SAID TO WAKE YOU."

I unfurled my body and sat up— a little too quickly; a wave of dizziness ambushed me. I let my legs dangle over the bed. Why did I feel like a rag doll? I remembered taking only one Librium. Yeah, but you took the adult dose, Dummy.

Having done her job, Audrey hopped on her bed. The stubby legs of a troll doll stuck out from under her pillow. She slid it out and stroked its wavy, popsicle-orange hair.

The mail.

"Did the mail come, Audrey?"

"UP-YAY," Audrey said with a sweet smile. "I BROUGHT IT IN MYSELF."

Crap. "Did Dad's letter come?"

"I DON'T KNOW. I JUST PUT EVERYTHING ON THE COUNTER."

I had to get myself downstairs. Maybe there was still time to swipe it. I made my way slowly down the stairs, leaning heavily on the railing. The TV was on in the living room. My mother was on the couch, engrossed in *The Edge of Night*. She didn't notice me slip into the kitchen. There, on the peninsula, in a teetering heap, was today's mail. A type-written envelope addressed to my father was perched right on top. I looked miserably at the return address: Raytheon, Dighton, Massachusetts. As if to chastise me, the clock over the fridge pointed squarely at 4 o'clock. Damn it. Surely, Mom would have looked through the mail. She's probably the one who put the letter right on top. My mission was so simple, and I blew it. The edges of panic prickled across my chest.

My mother called from the living room. "Finally, you're up." Startled, I knocked the whole pile over. "Why did you tell Audrey you would make her a Taylor Ham sandwich?"

"Umm," I said, re-stacking the mail into a neat pile. "I've seen Dad make them," I blurted.

She addressed the TV, "Stay away from the stove when I'm not home. Anyway, you kids made me buy Skippy peanut butter, so you better eat it," she barked.

"Ugh, Skippy's full of sugar," I mumbled under my breath.

"What'd you say?"

"Nothing." I needed time to think. "Can I go outside?" I cringed at having to ask permission, but I would need to stay on her good side.

"Yeah but don't disappear," my mother warned.

I've already disappeared from my old life, I thought to myself. "I won't. I'm just gonna sit on the front steps," I said to my mother.

"Oh by the way, while you were sleeping the afternoon away, Eve came by looking for you."

Eve. . . Eve! I hadn't thought about her in years. We walked to School 17 together every day singing "A Lover's Concerto" from that girl band, *The Toys.* Eve had a beautiful voice and wanted to be a singer. Eve had another talent too; she noticed things before others did. When I came down with the mumps in Mrs. Weiss' first-grade class, Eve knew something was wrong before I did. She sat in the next row, a couple of desks down from me. When Mrs. Weiss was busy underlining numbers on the hazy green chalkboard, Eve whispered, "Renee you got a lump under your ear."

That night back in first grade, I came down with the mumps and missed eight days of school. When Eve came to visit, she would sit on the back lawn outside the rec room window and talk to me through the screen like it was a confessional at St. John Vianney's. She said some of the kids didn't believe I was really sick. Someone saw me sitting on the front steps. I confessed that I sat outside after the fever went down. My mother said I could. When I was allowed back in school, the lump was still there but had shrunk to a small egg under my ear. I was glad, really. I went around showing the egg to the non-believers who conceded with grunts. After a month though, the egg was still there, and felt as though it was burrowing itself deeper into my neck. My mother said I was still healing. Eve said maybe a baby chick lived in it.

Absently I felt around under my ear. The egg was there, and it was tender. How was that possible? I had the mumps when I was 8, not at age 11. I pressed harder and winced. Just stay calm, Renee. You'll figure it out. Don't lose your shit.

Across the street, a girl hurried along the sidewalk and slipped into a front door. Was that Eve? Within minutes, a dirty, black Ford Falcon bumped up the driveway of the same house. A husky, balding man in blue work clothes and heavy black shoes got out of the car. Inexplicably, my chest tightened.

Then I heard the hollering and remembered. It was Eve's father, Mr. Caruso, who everyone steered clear of.

I tried to remember Eve's mother, but I couldn't conjure up a picture of Mrs. Caruso. However, something about her was percolating in my brain. Then like a parachute, the memory unfolded. It was during a sleepover at my house when Eve and I were 10. I was complaining about all the chores my mother had me do. Eve listened for a while and then whispered in the dark, "You're lucky, Renee. At least you got a mother." When I asked what happened to hers, she put her head under the pillow and mumbled, "My dad said she ran away and wasn't coming back."

Across the street, the Caruso house finally quieted down. The curtains were drawn as evening settled on Colonia. I missed Eve, but I better avoid her. She would sense that something was off with me. My mother came to the screen door. "Renee, come inside and set the table."

* * *

In between bites of fried chicken, my father gleefully read and re-read the Raytheon letter out loud:

> *Dear Joe,*
>
> *It was a pleasure meeting you last week at our Massachusetts plant. We know you would be a great fit for our Engineering team. I will call soon to set up a phone call with our plant manager.*
>
> *Very truly yours,*
>
> *Bill Davis*

My mother, always chatty during dinner, glared at my father. Yeah, Mom; I wish the letter was written in disappearing ink too. My father cleared his throat and mercifully folded up the letter and stuffed it back in the envelope. "So what did you do today, Hon?" he said, avoiding her glowering look.

Although the small fan whirled mightily from the kitchen counter, lifting the ends of our hair, my mother's blonde hair, coiffured into a beauty-shop flip and sturdy as a suspension bridge, remained freeze-dried in place. She put her fork down and continued her glaring. "Went food shopping, did four loads of laundry, got my hair done."

My father nervously rocked his can of beer. When he mustered enough courage to meet my mother's eyes, he gave her a what-do-you-want-me-to-say look. With a tight smile he offered, "Hair looks nice."

I glanced at my siblings. Audrey pushed her mashed potatoes around the plate. Kiel just stared into his glass of milk. "Can we go in the pool now?"

Kiel asked, stretching his thin legs out under the table.

My mother took a sip of her iced tea. "Good idea." She stood up, scraping the chair along the floor behind her. "Renee, it's your turn to clear the table." My mother then turned her back on us, yanked open the screen door, and walked down the cement steps to the yard, letting the door bang shut behind her. My father gave us an embarrassed smile and drained the rest of his beer.

After Audrey and Kiel changed into bathing suits and filed out to the pool with towels under their arms, I went to work scraping dishes into the garbage pail under the sink, grateful for a comforting chore in the quiet little kitchen. How was I going to fix this? Raytheon wanted him. I absently straightened up the dishes in the portable dishwasher. Then I caught myself and put a few plates in backward so my mother could fix them later.

I picked up Audrey's plate. Under her leftover mashed potatoes, Audrey had hidden her peas. I grinned. The adult Audrey still hated peas as well as most other vegetables. The kitchen wall phone rang. I answered it on the first ring, cherishing the heft of the clunky black handset. "Hello?" I said, coiling the long phone cord around me like a mummy.

"Hello there, little lady. Is your fa-tha home?" I knew this accent.

"Um, he's in the pool."

"Must be hot down there in New Joy-zee," he snorted. "Say, are you old enough to write down a message for me?"

"Yep," I said, rolling my eyes. I uncoiled myself and moved to the screen door. My mother, Kiel, and Audrey were drying off near the picnic table. My father was by the pool filter, tossing giant chlorine tablets into the pool.

Next to the phone was a pencil holder made from an empty frozen orange juice can. It was covered with scraps of construction paper and glossy pictures snipped from *Life* magazine. Inside the can were several pencils and a few broken crayons. Next to the juice can was a small stack of torn-up envelopes. I grabbed a chewed-up pencil and half of a Bamberger's envelope. "Okay, shoot."

"What?"

"What's the message, Mister?"

"Have him call Bill Davis. Okay, Sweetie? Here's the number: 508-824-4000."

It was him, the Raytheon guy my father met with last week. Back in last week, I was bickering with John over a storage unit. I jotted down the number while I craned my neck to spy on my family. My father had crossed the yard and was headed for the kitchen door. "Yup got it, bye," I said, cutting him off mid-sentence when he went on about reversing the phone charges. I hung up the phone and stared at the message scribbled by my 11-year-old hand. I had another shot at halting this chugging locomotive, yet this could stunt my father's career.

My father walked into the kitchen. I quietly squished the envelope in my fist. "Who was that on the phone?" he asked, reaching into the fridge for another Schlitz.

I stared at the back of my father's balding head while I felt for the garbage pail under the sink. I reminded myself that I would find him a better job right here. "Wrong number, Dad." And then I shoved the balled-up message down below Audrey's hide-the-peas concoction.

CHAPTER FOUR

I avoided Eve for a couple of days, first by locking myself in the basement bathroom when she called. When I saw her head up our front steps on the second day, I slipped out the kitchen door and hid in the cabana my father had built soon after we got the pool.

On the third morning, the smell of frying bacon jolted me awake like smelling salts. It must be Saturday which meant my father was cooking up his usual short-order-cook breakfast. I remembered the stories about his University of Maine summer breaks. He worked the snack bar at his uncle's motel in Camden, Maine. His uncle also had gas pumps out back. In between slapping burgers on the grill, my father would keep watch for cars pulling up to the pumps. When they did, he would whip off his apron, run through the back screen door, and pump their gas. After collecting their money, he would run back inside, tie up his apron, wash his hands (so he says), and flip the burgers over. I really missed his cooking.

I crept down the stairs in my cotton pajamas and watched him from the hallway. He zipped around the small kitchen, humming "Que Sera Sera." He confidently flipped pancakes in one skillet while he poked at sizzling bacon in another. When he whirled around to whisk pancake batter in a big metal bowl, a few wisps of his short comb-over hair, carefully slicked down with Vitalis, waved defiantly above his head.

I slid into a kitchen chair. My father looked over his shoulder and smiled at me. "You're the first one up, Kitten. Ready for breakfast?"

Although I really wanted that black goodness percolating on the stove, I said, "Sure."

He put a sizzling plate of bacon and steamy pancakes in front of me and tousled my hair. He seemed overly chipper this morning, his usually quiet demeanor replaced by a pep in his step.

My mother walked into the kitchen without a word. She went straight to the stove and poured herself a cup of coffee. My father gave her a playful hip bump. She scowled and moved away from him. I was nearly finished eating when Kiel and Audrey took their seats at the table. My father took a seat next to my mother. "Who took a phone message from a Bill a few nights ago?" he asked, scanning our faces. Kiel shook his head, as did Audrey. Then everyone stared at me.

I scratched at a mosquito bite on my leg. "Oh yeah, Dad. It was me. I left the message on the counter. Maybe it got thrown out by accident." Technically, a part of it was true.

My mother looked skeptical, but my father's good spirits stood firm. "Well, no harm done. Bill called again, and I also spoke with the plant manager." He waited until my mother lit a cigarette before delivering his good news: "Well you guys, Mom and I have a big announcement. We're moving to Massachusetts!"

Kiel and Audrey popped their heads up. My mother took a long drag from her cigarette. My father continued, "I'll be going back up to Massachusetts early next week to meet some people."

Shit, Shit, Shit. I just got here. Now what?

* * *

I lingered at the breakfast table long after Kiel and Audrey had headed outdoors to roam the neighborhood. The move wasn't going to happen overnight. The house had to sell first. And then there was the home inspection. I'm sure I could flub that up.

My mother interrupted my thoughts with, "Did you two girls have a fight?"

"What? Who are you talking about?"

"Eve."

I was hoping to avoid Eve a little longer. "Oh, her? Nah, thought I would just help you around the house."

"Look. I don't know what you're trying to pull, but you're not getting a raise in your allowance."

"No, I'm good, Mom."

"What does that mean?"

"I'm not looking for extra money." I got up from the table and started loading the dishwasher.

"Hey, those are clean!" my mother barked. "Look, I want you outside today."

Before I could protest, Kiel appeared in the kitchen. Someone was standing behind him. "Look who I found?"

And there Eve stood with her straight brown hair parted on the side, held in place by a blue plastic barrette shaped like a butterfly. "Hey, Renee, where've ya been?"

Although I feared that Eve's well-honed intuition would expose my peculiar state of being, seeing her after more than fifty years made my heart flutter with joy.

* * *

Eve wanted to go down to the playground behind St. John Vianney Church, the same playground I had bounded across after a teacher's cigarette turned into a cell phone. My stomach churned, but I figured as long as we steered clear of School 17, I was safe. "Sure Eve," I said.

While Eve and I walked, she chatted about the new comic she had bought with her allowance. For doing all the housework and cooking, Eve got a measly dollar a week which she blew on comic books from Lake's candy store. Eve especially liked the *Journey into Mystery* series. I steered her towards the shortcut in the back of School 17, grateful that I still remembered where it was.

When we got to the playground, I took a seat on a wooden swing. Eve went straight to the monkey bars and hung upside down like a bat. I half-listened to her go on about the chimera in the comic she had just finished. As Eve rocked slowly by her hooked knees, her budding breasts played peek-a-boo under her billowy cotton top. I resisted telling her to cover up; she'd be shedding the cocoon of innocence soon enough. She interrupted her monologue to ask, "So how come you've been avoiding me?"

I gripped the swing chains and walked my feet backward under the swing as far as I could go. "Um." What was I going to tell her? I died and then bubbled up in the backyard pool? She'd probably think I pulled that one right out of a comic book. I hurled the swing forward in a big underhand arc. The letter; I'll tell her about that. "My dad interviewed with a company up in Massachusetts."

"Groovy!"

I skidded to a stop in the dirt under the swing. "No, it's not. That means we'll have to move!"

"Oh, sorry. Yeah, that's not cool. I mean I just wish I could get out of here."

"You-" I caught myself before I blurted that she would. The flashback erupted from some deep fold of memory. My parents were hosting one last pool party before our beloved pool was taken down and sold. It was noontime. The hot dogs were on the charcoal grill, and the neighborhood kids were bobbing and splashing in our pool. Eve hadn't shown up, and we were about to do a whirlpool around the pool. The kids were lined up along the walls of the pool and were anxious to get the water rotated like a funnel. Eve wouldn't have wanted to miss it. The adults were huddled around the picnic table, listening to my Uncle Gene tell a joke. My mother didn't see me climb out of the pool and out the gate. I strode across the street dripping wet, rang Eve's doorbell several times and waited. When she finally opened the door, she was still in her pajamas, her hair hanging in a tangled brown cloud. She said she had been up late cleaning and overslept. I waited in the kitchen while Eve changed into her bathing suit. Then we headed back to my yard. I was about to open the gate when we heard my mother say, "You don't really believe that Juanita just up and left, do you?"

My hand froze on the gate latch. I looked over my shoulder at Eve, who pulled my hand away from the latch. She motioned for us to crouch in the grass and listen through a hole in the cedar fence.

My mother said that long before Eve was born, there was another daughter, Mary, who was married and expecting her first child. Mary drove to the Woodbridge station each morning to catch a train that would take her to her Advertising Assistant job in Jersey City. The year was 1951. Men were working nearby on the New Jersey Turnpike, constructing an exit for Colonia. To facilitate the turnpike project, the Pennsylvania Railroad had erected a temporary wooden trestle. But on February 6th, it had been raining all day. Packed with people heading home, the train derailed coming around a bend on the temporary trestle. Mary, just 18, her unborn baby and about eighty-four other people died.

Eve tapped me on the shoulder and nodded, indicating that she knew about the older sister.

"And you know, Bill was a heavy drinker even back then," my mother continued, stubbing out her cigarette. "I'd go over there to see Juanita, and there he'd be, sitting at the kitchen table glaring at her, chain-smoking and drinking beer."

"Why was he so mad at his wife?" My uncle asked.

"Because Bill blamed her for Mary's death. He said Juanita encouraged Mary to take that 'cockamamie job,' as he put it. But that wasn't the worst of it."

From the corner of my eye, I saw Eve bow her head. I whispered, "Are you sure you want to hear this?" She nodded. I took her hand in mine, and we braced for what was to come next.

After beer refills were passed around the picnic table, my mother picked up her story. "So four years later, Juanita was pregnant with Eve, but instead of Bill being happy about it, you know what the bastard said?"

"What?" my uncle prodded.

My mother put a tanned hand on my uncle's arm. "Wait a minute, Gene." She twisted around and checked for kids within earshot. Eve and I looked too. They were all surfing along on the whirlpool's current, kid screeching when their cartoon-character floats collided. My mother turned back around to her expectant audience. "That son of a bitch told Juanita to get rid of it!"

Eve gasped. A neighbor sitting at the picnic table shot a look toward the gate. But Eve was already up and gone, running back to her house. I ran after her, but she shut the kitchen door in my face. And just like her mother, my best friend had vanished too.

* * *

"Renee, Renee. Earth to Renee," Eve paged from the monkey bars, snapping me out of my daydream. I squinted up at her. She had rolled herself up and was seated on top of the bars. "What were you gonna say?"

"Hey watch me jump," I said, hoping to distract her. She crossed her arms over her chest and waited. I pumped my legs and swung like a pendulum until

I was good and high. When I had her full attention, I let go of the swing chains and catapulted myself several yards across the playground, narrowly missing the see-saw. I stuck the landing perfectly and then extended my arms and legs like a hood ornament. The power of my young body surprised and exhilarated me. God, this place was magical. And I wanted Eve to stay here with me, forever. I'd find a way.

Suddenly I felt woozy, like I was underwater, looking up at a blurry world. Eve was saying something, but her words were muffled. "What?" I said weakly.

"Renee, you're bleeding."

"Where?" I managed to whisper.

"From inside your right ear. And you got that lump on your neck again," I heard her say. Then I fainted. When the world came back into focus, Eve was hovering over me, asking me what I was trying to tell her.

"I don't know. What was I saying?"

When my fogginess dissipated, Eve extended her hand and helped me up out of the dirt. "Something about being in Heaven."

My heart thumped a warning as Eve helped me over to the water fountain. The headache was back. Stay calm.

* * *

On the walk home from the playground, Eve kept pestering me about the Heaven comment. She wasn't going to drop it. I wanted to know what else

I had sputtered too, but then I didn't. I gave in. "So what did I say, exactly?"

"You said you were never gonna leave Heaven."

Shit.

"Eve, I don't know why I said that. I must've spaced out."

"Spaced out," she repeated. "Never heard that one. I like it!"

We walked along quietly, but I could tell by the way Eve was staring at the sidewalk that she was churning things over in her head. She stopped and turned to me. "It's not just that. You've been acting really weird."

My stomach tightened up. "Like how?"

"Well, the other night, when we were all catching lightning bugs on Paddy's front lawn, you wouldn't talk to me. You ran away every time I came up to you."

I didn't remember being out at night. At all. But the mosquito bites on my legs disagreed. And then this morning, there was an earthy smell in my bed. "I'm so sorry, Eve. I just haven't felt like myself lately." That was true.

Eve snorted. "You sound like your mother."

"No, I don't."

When we got to my house, I had no intention of telling my mother that I didn't feel well. Eve must have sensed this because instead of leaving, she followed me into the house and gave my mother a full report.

My mother called the doctor. I remembered that he made house calls. He came when I had the mumps. I had been lying on the couch in my cotton pajamas. Every time he reached into his black bag, I held my breath, willing him not to pull out a shot.

Apparently, this time I wasn't sick enough for him to make the trip. Damn it, the force field. I didn't know where the office was, but if it were on the other side of the overpass, I wouldn't make it. The VW would implode, or maybe it would be just me doing the imploding. "Mom, I'm fine. I don't need to see a doctor," I pleaded.

"You're going," she said, picking up her straw purse.

When I got into the backseat of my mother's VW, she gave me a confused look and said, "You are old enough to sit in the front, you know."

"That's okay, Ma. I'm feeling a bit queasy. I don't want to throw up next to you."

"Oh goodness, alright. There's an empty coffee can back there and some Kleenex. Lock the door."

I pushed the metal post down and then silently pulled it back up. Not only would it save my life, but it would also save hers. If we were headed toward the overpass, I would jump out at the set of lights.

We rolled down the driveway, then down Westminster Road toward School 17 and the overpass. My stomach churned. I closed a sweaty fist around the metal door handle. The set of lights was up ahead. I would do a drop and roll. I began to feel lightheaded. No, not now. Get your shit together. Through my fogginess, I heard beeping. Oh, God.

My mother mercifully took a right turn before the overpass. The beeping that I had heard was her turn signal. I let out a long breath. Jesus, close call. Still, I had to figure out what hocus- pocus was needed to break through this damn force field.

At the doctor's office, a nurse directed us to a small wood-paneled office that smelled like rubbing alcohol and stale cigarettes. There was a desk at one end and a leather examination table at the other. I hoisted myself up at the table and stared at the faded Norman Rockwell prints on the walls. My mother made herself comfortable in a leather chair next to the desk. She took out a gold-plated compact and a tube of lipstick and re-applied her tangerine lips.

I was deep into my second *Highlights* magazine when a white-haired, obese doctor brushed in. He ignored me. Instead, he addressed my mother, asking how long my ears had been bothering me.

While he schmoozed with her, I tapped my heels against the metal frame of the exam table just to annoy him.

My mother interrupted the doctor. "Stop that, Renee," she squawked.

The doctor turned around and looked at me as if I had just materialized somehow. Idiot. He grabbed an otoscope off the wall and poked around in my ears. I tried not to breathe in his garlicky smoker's breath. With his tobacco-stained hands, he felt around under my ear and neck. He pressed on the lump. I winced. "She's got Swimmer's Ear and a bad inner ear infection," he said right into my face. "And a swollen gland."

"Swimmer's Ear? She hasn't been in the pool for days," my mother protested.

She had a point. An ear infection, yes. That would explain the blood oozing from inside my ear and the woozy feeling, but Swimmer's Ear? I hadn't been in the pool since Kiel conked me on the head. That was the day; that crazy day I swam back to 1966. When was that? A few days ago? I remember diving into a pool. What was I doing before that? I took a deep breath and exhaled slowly. Come on, Renee, think. You were arguing with someone. A husband? Yes, you were married. His name was... Why can't I remember? I started to feel lightheaded again. No, don't faint here. I tried to pinch off the panic before it took hold.

"She's as white as a ghost," the doctor said to my mother. "Why don't you lie back, little lady, while I talk to your mom."

I laid back on the examination table. What was my husband's name? My mind came near the horizon of a memory and just hovered there. It was like knowing the words to a hit song but not the title. Then I got angry. Those memories are mine. They shouldn't be taken away.

The doctor waddled over to his desk and scribbled out two prescriptions. He tore them off his pad and handed them to my mother. "She needs to stay out of the pool for a week."

On the way back, I tried not to think about "the before." You're here now where you always longed to be. And losing some of your future-life memories is the trade-off. This must be Nature's way of shedding your old life so that you can begin anew. In time, you will be fine. I held on to that buoy as I wept silently in the back of my mother's VW.

* * *

My mood brightened when we turned down Lake Avenue, and my mother rolled up to Dell's Pharmacy. I had forgotten that my beloved Lake's candy store was right next door. I had the car door opened before my mother pulled up the parking brake.

"Uh-uh. You stay in the car. I don't want to have to drag you out of Lake's."

"But, Mom-."

"I SAID, stay here. Why do you always have to give me an argument?"

I certainly would have argued the point, but I reminded myself again that I was 11. Eleven-year-olds were expected to shut up and behave, so I stayed in the car while my mother went into the pharmacy. Sooner or later, she would dole out the 25-cent allowances anyway. And then Kiel, Audrey and I would dash down to Lake's to spend it all on Bazooka bubble gum, Bonomo Turkish Taffy, and comics, like we always had. Funny how I could remember such mundane things from my distant past but couldn't remember my husband's name, where I lived, or when I graduated from high school. It seemed as though I could only remember people and places if they originated in New Jersey. After that, my mind's memory file was shredded, leaving only thin fragments. I felt my chest tightening again. Come on, get a grip. I climbed over the front seat and clicked on the radio to distract myself, thankful that my mother had left the keys in the ignition. Rolling the radio dial, I found WABC out of New York City. The station was re-airing a 1965 Beatles interview with the radio host, Cousin Brucie. I cranked up the volume. The nasal voice of John Lennon brought a smile to my face, then my mood darkened, but I didn't know why.

A boy on a bike whizzed by my open window. He jumped the curb of the parking lot and curled his bike to a smooth stop in front of Lake's. I slumped down in the seat. Did I know this boy with light brown hair and dark-rimmed glasses? I studied the Schwinn Wasp parked in front of the store. It had an old wooden cigar box attached to its back fender. A memory pinged in my cluttered brain; the bike belonged to JP, who lived around the corner from me.

I remembered that JP had an enterprising racket going. Along with your *Independent-Leader* newspaper, you could also get a side order of cigarettes delivered right to your front steps. Parents would leave notes and money for JP in their galvanized metal milk boxes. He knew what everybody smoked by heart and liked to spin off brands by household. "Mr. Gordts smokes Camels; Mr. DeLaune smokes Winston Menthols. Mrs. DeLaune smokes Salems, even though she tells everyone she quit. And Mr. and Mrs. La France smoke Pall Malls." JP said that Mrs. Camerucci didn't have a milk box. Instead, she'd come to the front door wearing a short, mint green negligee. JP would swish his thin hips and say, "And Mrs. Cama Roochie Coochie likes her Kools."

The store owner, Mr. Doto, who emigrated from Italy, was all for the cigarette delivery service. He supplied JP with the cigar box from his backroom saying, "Here son, so you don't-a- go-a flying over the handlebars steering with the one-a-hand."

* * *

When I heard Lake's screen door whap close, I straightened myself back up on the seat. For a few minutes, I watched boisterous kids loaded down with comics and candy exit the store. JP came out carrying a short stack of his wares. I poked my head out the window. "Hey, JP!"

I had startled him. "Oh, hi. I thought that was your mother's VW." He pushed up his thick glasses with his free hand. "Eve's inside reading comics." He tossed the cigarette packs into his cigar box and walked up to the car window. "Hey, why were you down by the creek last night in the middle of the night?" he whispered.

"What?" I squeaked louder than necessary.

"I got up to pee. I saw you."

My heart quickened. "It wasn't me, JP. You must've been dreaming."

"You were in your pajamas."

How the hell could I have been down there and not know it? But I couldn't explain that funny smell in the bed and all those mosquito bites on my legs. My mother was coming out of Dell's Pharmacy. I had to get rid of him. "I snuck out, JP, okay? Don't tell anybody."

He rapped his knuckles on the car twice. "Cross my heart and hope to die," he said, making a cross sign on his chest with his finger. Then with a wink, he got back on his bike, nudged up the kickstand, and disappeared up Cameo Place.

My heart crinkled over like a crushed beer can. I remembered something else about JP. He would die before he punched through 20. Not from flying over handlebars but through the windshield of a car with no seatbelts. Should I tell him? Would there be consequences to wiggling Fate? Well, I was here, wasn't I? And I sure as hell would be wiggling Fate, not just with my own life but with my whole family's and maybe Eve's. What's one more person? Yes, I would find a way to warn him.

CHAPTER FIVE

When my mother and I got home, I scooted right upstairs to my room. I tossed my bedsheets aside. The smell was gone, but there at the foot of the bed was a squished-up dead bloodsucker.

I picked up the bloodsucker and tossed it into the toilet. There was the proof; I was down at the creek. That meant I had slipped out of the house, crossed Westminster Road, passed through Paddy McGill's backyard, and crossed all four lanes of busy Jordan Road to make it to the creek. And then I had to get back.

My mother came up the stairs with ear drops. "Renee, grab the cotton balls and go lie down on your left side."

I flushed the toilet. The black creature swirled around in the toilet's whirlpool and then disappeared. I made myself comfortable on the bed. Audrey hovered by the bedroom door and watched my mother squeeze out the eardrops.

"Stay lying on your side until I say you can get up," my mother instructed.

After my mother left, Audrey came around the bed and tipped her face down to mine. Through my cotton-clogged ear, I heard her muffled, "DO YOU WANT SOMETHING TO PLAY WITH?"

"Nah."

"YOU CAN HAVE MY 8-BALL. YOU CAN KEEP IT."

My heart shot off a warning flutter. She loved that toy. "Why, Audrey?"

Audrey straightened herself up. "BECAUSE."

Before I could respond, she had moved away from the bed and out of my field of vision. I thought she had left, but then I heard the closet door slide open and bang to a stop. I lifted my good ear off the pillow. Audrey seemed to be rummaging around in the closet. She came back around and plunked the 8-Ball down next to my face. "HERE. I DON'T LIKE IT ANYMORE."

I sat up. The ear drops quickly seeped around the cotton and dribbled down my neck. "Audrey, what's wrong?"

Audrey's bottom lip quivered. "I ASKED THE BALL IF I WAS GONNA DIE!" Her eyes brimmed with tears. "AND IT SAID YES!" She bolted from the room before I could tell her no, she wasn't going to die down here in New Jersey.

Audrey's milestones clicked by in my mind like slides on a View-Master reel. She graduated from High School; I remember my mother complaining that her graduation dress was too short. College? Yes, she went to Bristol Community College in Fall River, Massachusetts, with the rest of us. Sure, she had a heart murmur, but she grew out of it. Yep,

Audrey was alive and present, growing old along with Kiel and me.

Those memories of Audrey, Kiel and me were so vivid, yet I still couldn't recall who I married or if I had children. I was locked behind my own iron curtain, unable to reach the Radio Free realm of forbidden recollections.

I picked up Audrey's 8-Ball. "Did I have a husband?" I gave it a half-hearted shake.

Ask again later.

"Yeah, right, but you have the time to mess with Audrey."

My reply is no.

"You better not be," I mumbled. I toyed with the 8-Ball some more. Earlier, it never confirmed if this was Heaven, so I asked again. "Am I in Heaven?"

Signs point to yes.

My heart bleated out a few jittery pumps. It wasn't quite a yes, but the needle had undoubtedly moved in that direction. I rolled the 8-Ball around in my hand. This was just a crazy toy. But I wondered if everyone who made it to Heaven got some sort of sidekick in their go-bag. The 8-Ball seemed to be mine. Perhaps it could help me with that troublesome force field on the overpass. If I had landed here for a redo, I would need to move about freely and not explode, trying to cross to the other side of Colonia. Many of the town's establishments were on the other side of the overpass. I had to break down the damn thing, and soon. "Can the force field be destroyed?" I gave the 8-Ball a hearty shake and turned it over.

Outlook not so good.

Shit. Then there had to be a way through it. I also needed to know why I was down at the creek. A faint aroma of pasta and garlic and tomatoes floated into the bedroom. My mother yelled up the stairs for me to come down. I rolled the 8-Ball under my bed and headed for the kitchen, to my family, and to the rest of my future past. I would deal with the force field and the creek excursion on a full stomach.

CHAPTER SIX

Since I was banned from the pool for the next several days, my mother took pity on me and let me go to the playground while everyone took an evening dip. I told her that some kids were building a fort down there. Although this was true, I had no intention of going there. "JUST BE HOME BEFORE IT GETS DARK," she shouted from the pool.

The sun hovered low in the trees when I passed by the schools and the playground. Up ahead was the Inman Avenue overpass. I could hear the cars wiz by on the Garden State Parkway below.

I stepped onto the overpass. The bridge was quiet, although I knew the force field would be lying in wait for me out there in the middle. I couldn't remember exactly where, though. Damn, I should've marked the spot. Tonight I would. There was a loose chunk of blacktop lying on the edge of the roadway. I picked it up and walked slowly, one foot in front of the other, as if on a tightrope.

I had only gone a few yards when my forehead and shoulder hit the force field. What the hell? Just a few days ago, the force field was out there in the middle. It had moved. The impact caused me to teeter backward, and for a moment, I caught a glimpse of the hazy barrier wiggling like a translucent Jell-O mold. I tightened my grip on the chunk of blacktop and chucked it at the force field. It sailed clean through it. Although I expected this would happen, seeing the rock go through shocked me. "Why won't you let me pass?" I snarled.

Something beeped. I put my ear up against the force field and waited. There it was again, like a faint pulse.

"Renee, what are ya doing?"

I whirled around. It was Eve. "Were you following me?"

"Who you talking to?"

"Nobody. What are you doing here?"

"I went by your house. Your mom said you were down at the playground, but you weren't. I saw you crossing the church parking lot, so yeah, I followed you."

Sweat began to bead up on my forehead. "Well, you can just turn around and go home," I said in a fluster.

"Not until you tell me what's going on. Why were you throwing that rock?"

But I couldn't tell Eve. She was only 11. I couldn't tell anyone. And who would believe me? They were still locking people up in insane asylums back in the 60s and zoning them out on Valium or Thorazine. So I said, "I'm fine, Eve. I just want to be alone."

Eve studied me for a moment, coiling her hair tightly around a finger. Then she walked ahead of me.

The force field.

Before I could react, Eve walked cleanly through it. She peered over the chrome guard rail at the cars rushing below. "Were you gonna jump?"

"No!"

"Then what? You better tell me— or."

"Or what? you'll tell?" I whined.

Eve put her hands on her hips and gave me an annoyed look. "Do I look like someone who'd tell a grown-up?"

The sun had slipped below the horizon, giving way to an ominous twilight. Eve was making me nervous, standing there on the backside of the force field so close to the knee-high guard rail. Headlights were coming on from the cars below. "Eve, let's just go home," I said, motioning for her to follow me.

From Eve's perspective, I understood why she didn't trust adults. Her parents had indeed failed her. Her mother had vanished, leaving Eve to ride out an uneasy childhood with a bitter father.

Eve walked towards me, passing back through the force field. It beeped, this time like a metal detector. She glanced behind her. "Did you hear that?"

I felt Adrenalin rush through me. "Hear what?"

"That noise, like a beep." Eve looked behind her and above. She took a step back through the force field. "There it goes again. Come see for yourself."

"I gotta get home." I turned to leave, but Eve grabbed my arm and pulled me forward. My shoulder bounced against the force field, and I fell backward onto the pavement. For the second time that day, Eve stood over me. Only now, she was screaming. "WHAT. IS. GOING. ON!"

I hollered back at her that I didn't know.

* * *

A car lumbered across the overpass from the far side. It stopped a few yards in front of Eve and me. The headlights were too bright to make out the husky, shadowy figure stomping toward us.

"What the hell are you two up to now?" a man bellowed.

Eve lowered her eyes. "We were just horsing around, Dad."

"I should knock some sense into you. Get in the damn car."

Mr. Caruso didn't extend the ride home to me, but with my heart racing, I followed Eve into the back seat anyway. If he were going to throw a backhanded blow or worse, I'd block it. Then I'd gouge his eyes out. It was my fault that Eve was out here.

The smell of stale tobacco and mildew choked the air out of the car. The black vinyl upholstery was dry and cracked like a fisherman's face. Wedged under the driver's seat were several crushed cigarette packs and empty beer bottles.

Mr. Caruso got in the driver's seat. There was a tinkling of glass bottles. I peered over the front bench seat. A six pack of beer peeked out from a paper bag on the floor. He bent over, and rearranged a couple of *Playboy* magazines inside the bag.

My chest gave off a warning squeeze. Would he try something with Eve? She never mentioned anything, but how many young girls did? I had hoped to ditch Eve, hide out inside my house, and cook up a story about the force field that she would believe. Surely she would demand that I explain the overpass phenomenon. But now? No, I couldn't leave her with that goon of a father. I waited until he sat back up and started the engine. "Mr. Caruso, is it alright if Eve slept over?"

He frowned at me from the rearview mirror. "I don't know about that. She left a pile of dishes in the sink. She's getting lazier by the day."

"It's my fault, Mr. Caruso. I made her come down here." Eve shot me a look. She opened her mouth to speak, but I squeezed her hand. "I'll tell you what. If you let her sleep over, I'll come over tomorrow and help her clean the whole house."

Mr. Caruso glanced at the bag on the floor, then back at me. "As long as she can behave herself." He switched his sneer to Eve. "Be nice to get her out of my hair for a night."

* * *

I wasn't sure how my mother would react to Eve sleeping over, but she was cool with it. She didn't complain about me getting home after dark. Maybe she took pity on Eve. Maybe my mother knew more than I did. "Just don't stay up all night," was all she said.

Eve and I headed down to the rec room. We could hear Albert and Kiel doing magic tricks. We sat down on the bottom step and watched.

"Now you see it," Albert said, displaying a quarter in his palm. He made a jerky movement with his arm and opened his palm again. "Now, you don't."

"I can still see it," Kiel said, pointing to the coin under Albert's thumb.

Eve and I exchanged a glance and then burst out laughing. When we settled down, Eve poked me in the shoulder. "So, are you going to tell me what happened on the overpass?"

"First, tell me what's going on with your father."

Eve's cheeks flushed. "Nothing."

"What's with the *Playboy* magazines?"

She shot me a surprised look. "Oh, those. He just shuts himself in his room with those girly magazines and his beer."

"Is he messing with you?"

Eve stared at her feet. "What do you mean?"

I put my arm around her shoulder. "Is he touching you...funny?"

She shook off my arm. "Noooo!"

"You would tell me, right?"

"I guess. Now it's your turn."

I pretended to watch Albert attempt the disappearing coin trick again. The coin flipped out of his hand and spun like a top on the black and white tiled floor. I wasn't about to tell Eve that I was, you know, dead, but I had to give her something. "You read a lot of comic books, right?"

"Yeah."

"Were there any stories about someone with a split personality?"

"You mean like Dr. Jekyll and Mr. Hyde?"

"Sort of. If I tell you something, you promise not to tell anyone, Eve?"

"I won't. I promise."

I told her that it wasn't me who made the comment about never wanting to leave Heaven at the playground. Eve's forehead crinkled up. I continued. "And then JP said he saw me down at the creek in the middle of the night."

She stared at me. "You're kidding, right?"

"Nope. That's why I've been acting weird. The other personality takes over sometimes."

Eve was buying this shit? Good. She looked thoughtfully at the floor. "So who's this other person, anyway?"

"I don't know."

Eve didn't say anything for a long time. I held my breath. My explanation didn't account for the force field or the beeping on the overpass. Shit. We watched Albert fumble the coin trick for the third time. Finally, she slapped her knee. "I got it!"

"What?"

"We can use Albert to find out who's inside you."

I let out a long breath. Eve surprised me. Although she was willing to believe my story, she was too much of a skeptic to fall for magic, and the last thing I needed was more exposure. "I don't want anyone else to know."

"Don't you want to know?"

She had me. Crap. I felt like I had fallen through a trap door. I glanced at Albert. "But he's terrible. Look at him."

"Yeah, I know, but he's got another talent."

CHAPTER SEVEN

I couldn't imagine what mysterious talent Albert had acquired that could possibly impress Eve. "Like what?" I asked.

Eve motioned over her shoulder. "Can we go up to your room?"

"Sure."

Once we had flung off our flip-flops and sat cross-legged on my bed, Eve said that Albert's mother had required him to read three books over the summer vacation, and none of them could be about magic.

"Boy, that must have made him mad."

"Yes Siree Bob. So when she drove him to the Woodbridge Library, he picked out three books on hypnotism. His mother was annoyed, but hey, a deal's a deal."

I uncoupled my legs and sat up straight. "So, is Albert any good?"

"He's getting better. He had Paddy McGill barking like a dog. That's what Paddy's sister said anyway."

Why would Eve believe this? Albert couldn't get through a simple coin trick. Paddy was either tricked into believing he had barked under hypnosis or was faking it. I grinned. Either way, this would work for me. "So you think Albert could draw out the other personality?"

"What do you got to lose?"

* * *

Albert was dragging a pock-marked metal trash can overloaded with garbage down his driveway when Eve and I intercepted him. I remembered that Albert secretly liked Eve, so I let her do the talking.

"You want me to do what?" Albert asked her.

"We want you to hypnotize Renee."

"What for?"

Eve explained to Albert that I had a split personality, and we wanted him to contact the other person. Albert grabbed the can's metal handle. "You girls are Looney Tunes."

We flanked him on each side as he dragged the can to the curb. "Whoever inhabits Renee's body made her go down to the creek in the middle of the night," Eve said.

Albert stared at his feet and absently skimmed a hand over his blond crew cut. Kiel had mentioned that Albert was saving up for a magician's cape. "Come on, Albert. I'll even pay you," I prodded.

Albert put his hands on his hip. "How much?"

I remembered seeing a pink ceramic piggy bank on top of the dresser. I had no idea how much money was in it, but Eve moved in to close the deal. "Five dollars."

"Meet me in the treehouse in an hour."

* * *

On the way back to my house to raid the piggy bank, Eve suddenly stopped. "Uh, Oh."

"What?"

"We forgot to clean my house. My dad will think we tricked him into letting me sleep over."

"I got this," I said.

"What do you got?"

"Never mind. Let's go to your house right now."

When we got to Eve's house, breathless from running, she reached under a lackluster rhododendron bush next to the front door and retrieved a key.

Like all the homes in the development, Eve's living room was situated on one side of the small entryway, with the kitchen on the other. Although the layout was identical to mine, the place gave off a gloomy, unfamiliar aura. There were no family pictures on the living room walls or frilly curtains in the kitchen window, and it smelled. Was it always like this?

I pointed to the sink full of dishes with stuck-on food. "Fill up the sink with hot soapy water. While they're soaking, go around the house, open all the windows, empty the ashtrays and trash cans, then just pick up the living room."

"That's not cleaning."

"No, but it will LOOK like we cleaned."

Eve grinned. "Groovy."

While Eve sprinted around the house, I pulled out an old Electrolux vacuum and zipped around the living room, making a few noticeable tread marks here and there on the threadbare grey carpeting. When I was done in the living room, I hefted the vacuum cleaner up the stairs.

I vacuumed my way down the dark hallway to Eve's bedroom. The shades were pulled up, and her bed was neatly made. Eve's desk was positioned under a sunny window overlooking a poured concrete patio and backyard. On the corner of the desk was a stack of comic books. If I had a father like hers, I'd lose myself in a fantasy world, too.

On my way out of Eve's room, I noticed that her top dresser drawer was open. I absently closed it. Something nagged at me. I turned the vacuum off so I could hear Eve if she came up the stairs. I slid the dresser drawer open. Inside were Eve's Minnie Mouse cotton underpants stacked in neat piles like pancakes. However, on one of the piles, a couple of underpants were upside down and askew. I closed the drawer again. Eve was meticulous about her drawers, but maybe she was in a hurry. I turned the vacuum cleaner back on and headed toward the stairs.

I couldn't shake the split-screen image of Eve's underwear drawer and the *Playboy* magazines in her father's car. Eve said not to go into her father's room, but at the very least, I owed it to Eve for drawing her into my mess. I nosed the vacuum cleaner into his room.

The shades were pulled down, and the darkened room smelled like BO. When my eyes adjusted to the dim light, I saw a once-white chenille bedspread and a top sheet on the floor in a tangled mess. A rumpled stack of girly magazines and a few empty Schlitz beer bottles were on the bedside table. A pigsty for a pig.

I held my breath, lifted the foul bed linens and looked under; nothing on the floor. I knelt and peeked under the bed. Between the tufts of dust was something white that looked like underwear. I pulled out a pair of Men's briefs. Ewww. I slid them back under with my foot. I checked behind the bedboard. A wooden frame was leaning against the wall. I reached down and pulled up a black and white wedding picture of Mr. and Mrs. Caruso. They were standing on the top steps of St. John Vianney church, smiling at each other.

I remembered that after school, Mrs. Caruso always waited for Eve on the sidewalk in front of their house. When she spotted Eve, she would crouch down with outstretched arms, ready for a hug. Then one day, she wasn't there. When her father got home from work, he told her that her mother had run off. "Where did you go, Mrs. Caruso?" I whispered at the picture.

The phone on the bedside table rang, startling me. I dropped the picture. Damn it. Although I could have used more time to snoop around, if Eve heard the thud, she'd be headed up here any minute. As I put the picture back behind the bedboard, I noticed a small dent in one of the corners. Shit, did I do that? Maybe it had been there before. I hoped so. If it wasn't, and Mr. Caruso noticed the dent, he would probably interrogate Eve.

We met back in the kitchen. I washed the dishes slowly. My mind focused on a new split image: Minnie Mouse underwear and crumpled whitey tighties.

"Who was on the phone?" I asked.

"Wrong number. Hey, where'd you learn to clean like this?" Eve said, putting away a bowl.

"YouTube."

Eve gave me a skeptical look. "What?"

Shit. Keep it together. "I mean the boob tube." I pointed to the clock over the sink. "Come on, let's get going. Albert's probably pacing up there in his treehouse."

* * *

On the walk back to Albert's, I pondered who I would conjure up under hypnosis. Eve loved *The Patty Duke Show*. She never questioned the show's crazy premise that the identical twin fathers spawned the identical twin cousins, Patty and Cathy, both parts played by Patty Duke. So I picked the demure, "identical" cousin, Cathy, to emulate. Eve would be intrigued, and hopefully, the disarming Cathy would stroke Albert's ego.

When we got to Albert's backyard, we hurried up the ladder to the treehouse. Albert was sitting on the plywood floor with his back against one of the chest-high walls of the structure. He was reading a book. On his head was a bright orange bath towel wrapped like a turban. Albert had pinned his mother's costume jewelry ruby broach to the center of the turban. I cupped a hand over my mouth to stifle a laugh. He looked nervous. Good. He shut the book when he saw us.

Eve let out a snort. "Albert, would you please take that stupid towel off your head?"

"Yeah, sure, sorry," he said, unraveling his turban. "Are you ready, Renee?"

"I guess so."

"Sit there." Albert pointed to a bunched-up army blanket on the floor near the back wall of the treehouse. The blanket was scratchy and smelled mildewy. A moth lazily fluttered away when I picked it up to shake it out. Albert sat on his knees in front of me. "Okay, let's begin. Now, I want you to relax, Renee. Take a couple of deep breaths. Focus on my voice."

Albert reached into his pocket and pulled out a brass pocket watch on an old chain. He swung the watch back and forth in front of my eyes. "This is ridiculous," I said, crossing my arms over my chest. I wasn't going to make it that easy for him.

Albert straightened up and put down the watch. "It's not going to work if you fight it. You have to BELIEVE that it will work."

"Come on, Renee, concentrate," Eve prodded.

"Alright, alright. Go ahead, Albert; I'm ready."

Albert picked up the watch again. In a soothing voice, he told me that I was getting very, very sleepy. I closed my eyes slowly and slumped my shoulders dramatically. Up next would be Cathy Lane. I thought about giving her an English accent.

Albert continued, "Renee, can you hear me okay?" In a sleepy voice, I responded that I did.

"Now, Renee, on a count of 3, I'm going to snap my fingers. When I do, I want you to go to sleep so we can talk to someone else."

I slumped down a little further and waited for Albert's cue. I heard a slight swish of leaves from the massive oak tree that cradled the treehouse. Soon a gentle breeze drifted down over the plywood walls. It swept across my shoulders, circled my legs, and then gently lifted me up and out of the treehouse. I drifted above the trees, cocooned in the warmth of a mother's womb. I slept. I dreamt that I was in a small room. On a bed? Yes. Near me was a white box that beeped. A blurry figure leaned over me. The figure said something, but I couldn't decipher the words.

Abruptly, my dream shut off. There was a muffled voice, insistent and nervous. Someone was telling me to wake up. It sounded like Eve. The womb dissipated around me.

"Albert, you can't leave. You have to get her back," I heard her say.

"I can't. I don't know how."

"For Christ's sake, gimme the damn book," Eve said.

With great effort, I opened my eyes. Eve was shaking my shoulders. "Renee, are you okay?"

"Yeah, I think so." Behind her, something caught my eye. It was Albert, rapidly descending the ladder. "Where's Albert going?"

Eve rolled her eyes. "He's scared. Scared of you."

I felt a little queasy. "Why, what did I say?"

Eve let out a long breath and then settled down next to me. She handed me a thermos bottle. "Albert's mom made some Kool-Aid. Want some?"

"Sure. Now tell me what I said, Eve."

While I chugged the Kool-Aid, Eve stared off, absently twisting her hair. The sky had clouded over, and soon a furious rainstorm pelted the roof of the treehouse. I nudged her. "Come on, Eve. What happened?"

Eve's eyes met mine. "Well, Albert was about to give up when all of a sudden, you opened your eyes and punched him in the chest."

"What? Why?" I had no memory of actually impersonating the ladylike Cathy Lane, but if I had, she wouldn't be throwing a punch. So who the hell came through?

"Let me finish. So Albert says, 'Why'd you hit me,' and she goes, 'Because you woke me up.'"

"I said that?"

"Yeah, but it wasn't you, you. I mean it was you, but you sounded like a first-grader."

My mouth went dry. I took another swig of Kool-Aid. Albert was supposed to bomb. I needed to know precisely what Eve knew, and now Albert. Stay calm. "That must have really spooked Albert. So what else did I say?"

"Albert kept asking what her name was and how old. She wouldn't say. Then Albert bribed her with a lollipop."

Each Halloween, Albert hid his candy in a different spot so his sisters wouldn't eat it. Maybe it was the treehouse this time, and only the lollypops were left.

"Finally, she said her name was Missy, and she was eight years old."

I felt light-headed. "Missy?"

"Yeah, so we asked her why she was sleeping in your body." I braced for impact. "She started crying and said she didn't know."

"Did she say what she wanted?" I put my shaking hands under my legs so Eve wouldn't see.

Eve's eyes glistened with fascination. She seemed intrigued by the whole thing as if this was just another comic book mystery adventure. "Nope. So we asked Missy how she got here."

"And?" I asked.

"She said she came with you."

"That's impossible!" But as I said it, a vague recollection of being underwater bobbed around in my head. I closed my eyes and concentrated. Soon an in-ground pool materialized in my mind, then a string of images lined up like dominoes: a diving board, a drain at the bottom of the pool, my diving into the pool, and finally being sucked into the drain —no, pulled into the drain by someone. No, it can't be. Missy? Oh, God.

"There's more."

"What?"

"She said she wasn't leaving."

A cold sweat spread across my back. The bloodsucker in my bed, the midnight romp through yards, was that confirmation of Missy? I staggered to my feet, bent over the treehouse wall, and threw up red Kool-Aid.

* * *

The heavy rain dwindled to a constant drizzle. Eve allowed me to recover from vomiting before she started her interrogation. "So Renee, who's Missy?"

I needed time to think. If I had drowned in a past life, I would have eventually floated to the top of the pool, not pulled down the drain by someone named Missy. But why? What did she gain by being here? It also meant that I didn't bring her here; she brought me. I was just a vessel. Eve nudged me, but I ignored her. If I didn't drown, then I wasn't dead. Then what was I?

It started in my stomach, that sinking feeling like bottomless grief. It was clear; this wasn't Heaven. Then where the hell was I? Eve nudged me again. I took a deep breath and faced her. Part of me wanted to yell everything out right then and there. Eve was fearless, wise beyond her years. She didn't scramble down the ladder like Albert. She wasn't scared on the Inman Avenue overpass either. Yet, if I spilled it all, would she believe me? I wouldn't believe me. However, I needed her help now. "Eve, there IS something I need to tell you."

Eve sat up straight and curled her arms around her knees. "I'm ready."

"Something extraordinary happened to me."

"Yeah, you can say that again."

"Eve, just listen."

"Okay."

"What I'm about to tell you probably won't make sense, and it's a little scary."

"Ooh, I'm shaking," she mocked.

"And you have to promise me you won't tell anyone."

Eve crossed her chest and chanted, "Cross my heart and hope to die. Stick a needle in my eye."

"This is going to sound really strange, but I think that this little girl, this Missy person, came from somewhere else."

"Like from another state?"

"Well, not exactly from a physical state. More like a spiritual state."

Eve crossed her arms. "What do you mean?"

"What I mean is, I think she sort of invaded me."

Eve smirked. "How?"

"My memory is kind of sketchy, and maybe it was a dream, but I think we were floating along in a water tunnel. And I think this is where Missy attached herself. I remember feeling a presence."

The corners of Eve's mouth began to twitch. She slapped her knee and let out a loud snort. "Oh, Come on! A water tunnel?"

"No, really."

"You had me going there for a while, Renee."

"I'm not joking."

"Why didn't you tell me this before?"

"Because I didn't think you would believe me, but now I really need your help."

"For what?"

"The force field. I think this Missy person was trying to warn me about the force field."

"What force field?"

"The one on the overpass. It won't let me pass, and it's moving in closer."

Eve's face darkened. She stood up and put her hands on her hips. "Come on, Renee. Why won't you tell me what's really going on with you? You weren't in a water tunnel. You faked it on the overpass, and I'm starting to believe you faked Missy." Eve grabbed the hem of her shorts and gave them an angry yank. "You had your fun. I'm going home. Find yourself another sap."

Eve headed down the ladder.

I scampered after her, knelt over the ladder, and grabbed Eve's shoulder. "Wait, Eve. Don't go. I admit I haven't been completely honest, but I'm not lying about Missy or the force field."

"Lemme go," she said, trying to shake my grip.

"But Eve, the force field beeped. You heard it." Eve wouldn't look at me, but she stopped struggling. "Eve, I swear to you, it's the truth."

"Alright, alright. We're going back to the overpass right now. I'm not saying I believe you, so you'll have to prove it. And then you're gonna tell me everything."

I released my grip. "Yes, that's a great idea. I'll go." I followed Eve down the ladder.

The rain had stopped. Patches of bright sun poked through the heavy cloud cover. We walked along the side of Albert's garage and out to the sidewalk. A thin figure was running towards us. He was shouting something. I shielded my eyes from the sun's glare. "Kiel?"

"Renee, where ya been?" Kiel yelled up the street. When he caught up to us, he stooped over to catch his breath. "We... we've been looking all..." he panted.

"Why? What's wrong, Kiel?"

"It's Audrey. She got rushed to the hospital."

CHAPTER EIGHT

On the way home, Kiel told us that Audrey had been skipping rope in the backyard. She was fine. A little while later, our mother came out to put sheets on the line. She found Audrey lying on the ground, unconscious and blue. As we neared the house, I noticed that the backyard gate had been propped open with one of my mother's black, heavy antique irons. "Kiel, did Mom go with Audrey?"

"Yeah, they let her ride in the ambulance."

"Did the EMTs give Audrey CPR?" Kiel gave me a confused look. "The medics, Kiel, what did they do?" I barked.

"They put her on a stretcher."

"Kiel, was she breathing?" I snapped back.

"I DON'T KNOW, RENEE!" he shouted back. "Everybody's down in the rec room, and Paddy's mom is on her way over. Mom said to stay home."

* * *

The rec room was full of kids. Albert, Paddy McGill, and JP huddled on the couch, talking quietly amongst themselves. Their sisters sat gloomily in a circle on the floor. Twin girls I vaguely remembered sat on the bottom steps. They parted so Kiel, Eve and I could pass. Everyone stopped talking and stared at us. The laundry room was at the bottom of the stairs to the right. I snuck in there to think. Eve followed.

What kind of weird time warp was this? Audrey was never rushed to the hospital. I remember Kiel going when he was about ten years old, but not Audrey. And Kiel didn't go by ambulance; my father drove him. It was during a game of "The Girls Catch the Boys." A pack of girls caught Kiel and dragged him through the back door of the garage, where he was supposed to remain a captive while we attempted to round up the other boys. Paddy McGill's sister, Amy, was standing guard outside the door when Kiel tried to escape. Just as he was charging through the doorway headfirst, Amy slammed the door on his head. The blow caused a concussion. When Kiel came home from the hospital, he was nauseous, so my mother put the yellow cleaning bucket next to his bed. After he fell asleep, we had to wake him up every two hours to ask him who the president was.

* * *

"Renee, are you okay?" Eve asked.

"This is all my fault," I blurted before realizing I had said it out loud.

"No, it's not. You weren't even there," she whispered.

Did I really want to suck Eve further into my mess? Once I did, there would be no turning back.

What choice did I have, though? People around me were getting hurt. I needed her help. "I don't think it was a coincidence that we exposed this Missy person, and then Audrey collapsed."

"No way. Missy's only eight, remember? She's harmless."

"Eve, Audrey might die because of me."

"Why, what did ya do?"

"I came back."

"Came back from where?"

"Some other realm."

Eve rolled her eyes. "Oh, not that again."

"Listen to me. I think there's too many of us here."

"What do you mean?"

"I tried to tell you about the water tunnel. I came through it, but I don't think Missy was supposed to. I think she was a stowaway."

"That's ridiculous." Eve turned and headed back to the vigil in the rec room.

I grabbed her shoulders and spun her around. "Eve, if Audrey was harmed because of Missy, you may be in danger too."

"Why? What did I do?"

My father had built a tiny half-bath off the laundry room. I herded Eve into it and shut the door. I sat her down on the toilet. "It's not what you did, Eve. It's that you exposed Missy. And you heard what she said. She wasn't leaving."

"Yeah?"

"Well, a few days ago, Audrey was very upset. She had asked her 8-ball if she was going to die."

"Why in the world would she ask that?"

"I don't know. Audrey wouldn't tell me. But get this, she asked the question, like three times, and each time it gave her the same yes response."

Eve crossed her arms. "I don't know, Renee, it's just a stupid toy."

"Well, that stupid toy also warned me about the force field."

Eve leaned against the toilet tank. "It did? What did you ask it?"

"If the force field could be destroyed. It said no."

Eve stood up and then lifted the toilet lid. She yanked down her shorts and underwear and sat back down to pee. "How does the 8-Ball know that?" she said, ripping off some toilet paper.

"Because I think it's Missy trying to communicate." There I said it.

Eve wiped herself and hiked up her clothes. Her eyes widened. "Through the 8-Ball?" Eve held her gaze while she reached back and flushed the toilet.

"Yeah. But every time I try to get more information, it just repeats the last response over and over, like it's in a loop."

Eve turned on the faucet. "Why would she do that?"

"Maybe she doesn't trust me."

"Then why communicate at all?"

"I don't know."

Eve dried her hands thoughtfully. "Maybe she warned you about the force field because she was scared of it, not because she was trying to help you. And maybe she warned Audrey because they're the same age. She felt safer."

I don't know if I was more stunned that Eve was coming around or that she had a pretty good working theory. Either way, I was grateful to have a confidant. "But if she's scared and figures out we're on to her, she'll clam right up."

"Well, then we'll just have to trick her," Eve said with a sly smile.

* * *

My father had met my mother at the hospital after she placed a panicky call to the plant. She also called Paddy McGill's mother and asked her to stay with us until they got home. By dusk, Paddy was the only one left in the rec room with Kiel and me. The others had gone home after Mrs. McGill called down to say that the street lights had come on, which to most kids, meant they had to go home. My mother had a different and very perplexing rule, open to interpretation: "Be home before it gets dark." I was never quite sure how fast twilight would fade into full nighttime, but I figured if I could still see figures running around on the lawn playing Hide and Seek, it must still be "before dark."

While we waited for news about Audrey, Mrs. McGill made us grilled cheese sandwiches and heated up canned tomato soup that she found in the cabinet. To further distract us, she set up metal TV trays so we could watch *Lost in Space*. Although the gooey Velveeta cheese sandwich was heavenly, I could only get through a few bites. I handed the rest of my sandwich to Paddy when I heard my father's Kingswood station wagon pull into the driveway.

The boys were engrossed in a scene where Penny Robinson confronted her mother and didn't notice me tip-toeing to the bottom of the stairs to eavesdrop. Soon I heard a scrape of a chair. Mrs. McGill asked about Audrey, and then my father cleared his throat. Upon hearing his mother's voice, Paddy's ears perked up and he nudged Kiel. Both boys shoved aside their rickety TV trays and stampeded up the stairs past me. They made such a clamor that I couldn't hear what my father had said to Mrs. McGill. Damn. So up the stairs I went right behind the boys.

My parents and Mrs. McGill were sitting around the kitchen table whispering. Audrey was not there. They stopped talking when we barreled into the kitchen.

"How's Audrey?" I asked.

The adults eyed each other. My mother spoke. "She sprained her arm and has to stay in the hospital a little longer to rest."

"Does she have a cast?" Kiel asked, settling down in a chair next to my father.

"Is she breathing on her own?" I blurted before realizing I had upended their cover story.

My mother's head shot up. She struggled to stay composed. "She has a sling," my father said.

"She's going to be fine. She's alright now. She'll be fine," my mother interjected in a shaky voice.

I couldn't help myself. "Are they running any tests?"

My parents looked at each other and then at me. "Yes, as a matter of fact, she'll be transported to Deborah Hospital in the morning for what's called a catheterization," my father said.

Kiel scrunched up his face. "On her arm?"

My father stared out the kitchen window. My mother swept up imaginary crumbs on the table. Neither of them responded, so I did. "No, it's for her heart."

"Renee!" my parents barked at me in unison.

"It's just a precaution. We don't know why Audrey passed out," my mother said. She rose from the table. "Look, it's been a long day. Why don't you kids get ready for bed."

I was too wired to sleep, but my parents certainly needed their space. I did go to my room but hovered near the doorway, out of view. I had a partial view of the living room from this vantage point. The phone rang. My father headed towards the couch while my mother answered the phone. She immediately began speaking rapidly in Italian. This meant she didn't want us to overhear what was said.

After the call, my mother joined my father in the living room. "I'll call Bill in the morning and tell him I can't take the job right now," my father said.

My mother reached for the crystal cigarette lighter on the coffee table. "And to think I scolded Audrey for laying around so much." She lit a cigarette.

"Come on, Hon. No one knew Audrey had a weak heart. The pediatrician certainly didn't pick it up."

A weak heart?

There was never anything seriously wrong with Audrey's heart. Was this some sort of sick trade-off, returning to my sacred Colonia for Audrey's heart?

My mother began to cry. My father's arm went around my mother's shoulders. "Hey, you got your wish. We can stay in Colonia."

My mother wailed louder. "Don't say that, Joe!"

I'm so sorry, Mom. I'm sorry, Dad. This is all my fault, and I'm going to fix it, I thought to myself.

* * *

When my parents headed up to bed, I quietly closed my bedroom door. It was late. From the open window, a slant of humid moonlight illuminated Audrey's empty bed. I had failed her. And this wasn't the first time.

When Audrey was four years old, Eve and I were walking to School 17, deep in conversation about the *I Dream of Jeannie* episode we had watched the night before. Behind us, a voice called out to me. I turned around; it was Audrey running to catch up to us. She had gotten out of the house without my mother knowing and had followed us. "I want to go to school with you!" she whined. I yelled at her to go home, then continued walking. When Eve and I rounded the corner onto Carolina Avenue, I heard Audrey calling out again. I ignored her. Eve was concerned and suggested that we bring Audrey home. She reasoned that we could still make it to school on time if we hurried. I told Eve no; Audrey would eventually give up and go home on her own. When Eve and I reached the school, Audrey ran up to me with a triumphant grin. I spun her around and hollered at her to go home. Then, I went inside the school.

During the Pledge of Allegiance, something outside caught Mrs. Einhorn's attention. When we finished the pledge, she asked us to remain standing. She pointed to the large bank of windows above the bookcases and said, "There's a little girl outside crying. Does anyone recognize her?" I knew it was Audrey. So did Eve. My classmates eagerly stampeded to the windows. Eve shot me a sympathetic look. JP pointed to Audrey and said that it was my little sister. I was embarrassed and angry. Mrs. Einhorn asked if I lived close enough to walk Audrey back home. I didn't want my mother to find out that I had abandoned Audrey in the schoolyard so I lied and told Mrs. Einhorn that I lived just down the street, hoping she wouldn't need to call my mother.

With the judgmental eyes of the third grade watching from the windows, I marched Audrey out of the schoolyard. Once away from the school, I scolded her on the sidewalk for embarrassing me in front of my class. Audrey started to cry. I told her not to be such a baby. I pointed her up Westminster Road, shoved her forward, then hurried back to school. Around noon, I walked home for lunch. There was a police cruiser in our driveway. I flew into the house in a panic. Audrey was sitting on the couch crying. A tall police officer with an overhanging belly told my mother that Audrey was found standing outside Lake's candy store. Apparently, in Audrey's distraught state walking home, she had overshot our house and walked another quarter mile to busy Lake Avenue. The officer noticed her standing in front of the store and pulled over. Audrey told the officer that a man had picked her up in his car and was inside the store buying her candy. I proclaimed loudly to my mother that I had brought Audrey all the way home but that she must have gotten out again. The officer eyed me suspiciously as my mother walked him to the front door. After my mother berated Audrey for getting into a car with a stranger, Audrey was too exhausted and upset to challenge my version of events.

The man in the store was never found. The suspicion was that he slipped out the back door when he saw the police officer through the store's front windows. After that day, the unrelenting guilt ate at me. I became Audrey's protector, the big sister I had never been before. I gave her a dime from my 25 cents weekly allowance for a month, hoping my guilt could be spent away.

* * *

And now Audrey was in the hospital because of me. I groped under my bed for the Magic 8-Ball. Eve said I should trick it; find out if it's Missy trying to communicate. I grasped the ball and settled onto Audrey's bed. If my presence had something to do with Audrey's heart condition, maybe Missy knew why. "Hey there, Magic 8-Ball. Are you awake?" I gave it a delicate shake and turned it over. A ghastly haze fogged the glass window on its underbelly. "Come on. I know you're in there. I just want to talk." Slowly, the fog began to clear. "Thank you." I made myself comfortable against Audrey's pillow, sliding her troll dolls out of the way. "Will you talk to me?" I gave it another gentle shake before turning it over.

Cannot predict now.

"Okay, that's fair, but look, I think we can help each other. I just need you to trust me. Will you do that?"

There was movement at the far end of the hallway, a flush of the toilet. Someone was up. Footsteps were coming down the hall towards my bedroom. There wasn't time to hop back to my bed, so I slid under Audrey's covers and slumped down a little on her pillow. I slid the 8-Ball under it. I closed my eyes and steadied my breathing.

There was a sniffle. I opened my eyes a sliver and saw my mother hovering over me. I waited for her to rouse me and tell me to get into my own bed, but she just stared at me. Maybe she wished it was me who had the heart condition, the middle child who constantly challenged her.

The mattress sunk a bit. My mother was sitting next to me. The smell of her hairspray lingered in the sticky air. She leaned over and swept hair off my brow. She had tolerated my backtalk, at least until my teen years, when we constantly fought over skirt lengths, boys, and chores. I clenched my jaw so as not to expose my grateful grin at her tenderness. Then my mother stood up. I snuck another peek. Her white nightgown fluttered around her knees as she moved away from the bed and out the door.

I sat back up and reached for the Magic 8-Ball under the pillow. The glass window on its underbelly had lapsed back to fog. I kept my voice to a whisper. "Come on back. Come on." I waited. I gave the 8-Ball a gentle swish. "Will you please trust me?"

Don't count on it.

"Understood. You're probably scared. I want to get to know you. Is your name Missy?" There was a pause, and then a **Yes** appeared. My heart banged against my chest. Was it really her? This is nuts. "Nice to meet you, Missy."

A tiny wave of fluid rippled across the glass. This was getting interesting. I had a million things I wanted to ask her. Perhaps she was lonesome, scared, or both, like Eve said. "Missy, I need your help. Do you know what happened to Audrey? I won't be mad. Did you have something to do with Audrey's heart condition?"

My reply is no.

"Come on, Missy. You can tell me."

The force field. Missy said to stay clear of it when Albert hypnotized me. On a hunch, I asked, "Is there someone or something trying to hurt Audrey?"

Better not tell you now.

It had dawned on me that I had stopped doing the customary shimmy shakes to erase the previous responses, but like a street sweeper, she was clearing them away on her own. "I don't think you meant for Audrey to get hurt. I just need you to answer one more question. Did the force field trick you?"

The street cleaning operation ceased. I tried shaking the ball. The better not tell you now answer remained frozen in place. I waited. "Okay, I know you're scared. If the force field tricked you, do that ripple thing again."

I stared hard at the ball, afraid to blink. A few minutes went by. I got off Audrey's bed and moved to the cone of moonlight coming from the window. I rechecked the 8-Ball. There was a slight movement, not really a ripple. I dismissed it as just my eyes getting tired. And then, like a tidal wave, the cloudy grey liquid rolled under the glass. There was no mistaking the signal. The force field was more than just a barrier. Whatever entity was controlling the force field was a threat, to Missy, to Audrey, and to me.

The moonlight disappeared under thick thunderstorm clouds. There was a rumble in the distance. The liquid in the 8-Ball settled. I asked

Missy if she would help me get rid of the force field. Again, I waited. There was no ripple this time. Getting sleepy, I lumbered back to my bed. I gave the 8-Ball a little shake. "Come on, Missy."

Slowly, in kid scratch, letters began to form like a developing Polaroid. Missy had a message for me: **Go home.**

CHAPTER NINE

I was too shaken up to sleep. The **Go home** message had floated under the glass for a few seconds, then dissolved like disappearing ink. What did she mean? And was my presence here hurting Audrey? I shook the ball repeatedly, trying to conjure Missy back, but the liquid remained cloudy and motionless.

Up to that point, the Magic 8-Ball responses were one of eleven standard wishy-washy answers built into the toy. **Go home** was not one of them. Was Missy a spirit? I didn't believe in ghosts, but here I was in the land of twisted time, force fields, and a hacked Magic 8-Ball. Missy had a point, though. I didn't belong here. That hope was extinguished back in 1966, the day the moving truck pulled away from this house. There would be no sleeping tonight.

The distant rumbles subsided. I crept out of the bedroom and listened at the top of the stairs. An ensemble of snores and humming fans drifted out from the bedrooms. I wondered how they could sleep in this heat and humidity. But then again central air was a modern luxury back in 1966. Middle-class Americans were grateful for their whirling fans.

I headed down to the kitchen. Go home, the message said. But I didn't WANT to go back. The nectar of this miraculous place seduced me the day I bubbled up from the bottom of the pool. And how would I actually get back? But there was Audrey. I was a threat to her. God damn it.

* * *

I was still banned from the pool because of my ear infection, so I couldn't sneak in it and search for an escape hatch during the day; I'd risk getting caught by Kiel, who enjoyed having the pool to himself. I unlocked the kitchen door and slowly turned the knob. The door was swollen and stuck. I pulled harder. The door opened, but the screen door complained with a suctioning rattle. I froze, straining to hear footsteps or my parents calling out. The house remained quiet. I stepped outside.

I walked across the yard. The cool, damp grass under my feet felt refreshing. The pool's metal frame glinted in a slice of moonlight. I loved this pool; there were so many happy memories of friends popping over on hot summer afternoons. The pool never made the trip to New England. My parents sold it before the move and didn't bother to tell us. However, the memory of the pool lived on in a life-long recurring dream where it was ceremoniously assembled by my father and brother each Memorial Day weekend.

But right here and right now, my old friend was waiting for me. My father always took the ladder out of the pool at night. It was standing next to the cabana, directly under my parents' window. If I moved the ladder, it would squeak and then make a splash when I placed it in the water. The pool was only shoulder height. Surely, I could scale it. I shed my baby doll pajamas on the grass, hoisted myself up, then eased into the pool.

The day's heat had warmed the pool to a tepid coolness. I could feel my heart racing. The clouds had moved on, leaving behind a big shiny moon. If someone went to the bathroom and looked out the window, they would surely see me. I waded to the center of the pool. Taking in a deep breath, I sunk into the blackness of the bottom, shutting out the world. It was just me down there. With one hand, I felt around the bottom of the pool and found the white plug. However, the plug was not flush with the liner. It was protruding slightly at an angle above the liner. Perhaps the force of my entry into this world had disturbed it. I tried to wiggle it back into place, but it wouldn't budge. I would have to pull the plug out entirely and then center it. I came up for air, took in a big long breath then plunged back under. I grabbed onto the plug and yanked. The plug popped open.

I expected to see a small circle of sand under the pool. Each year before erecting the pool, my father fastidiously smoothed out and leveled the sand. Instead, there was a deep, swirling blue whirlpool the size of a quarter. And it glowed. Holy shit! I quickly jammed the pool plug back in and surfaced. I vaguely recalled a water tunnel but not a tiny whirlpool.

The night sky had lightened. An eager bird chittered in the distance. I was running out of time. I took a big gulp of air and sunk back down. When I tugged on the plug again, the blue hole immediately began to expand like a giant throat, widening to the size of a dinner plate. A dead worm got swept up in the hole's whirlpool and disappeared. Tentatively I hovered my hand a few inches over the swirling phenomenon. The draw was weak, like a lackluster vacuum cleaner, too weak to draw in my hand. My chest tightened. If this was supposed to be my escape hatch home, it was a cruel joke. A moment later, the hole closed as if to say, "To hell with you then." Stunned, I jammed the pool plug back in, then launched myself to the surface. I took several deep breaths to calm myself.

In the twilight, I noticed bits of grass rimming the pool's walls. The water level had dropped a few inches. No! I looked around for the hose, thinking I could fill it before morning. I spotted the hose curled up below the faucet. It was right below my parent's window. If I turned the faucet on now, my father would hear the water running and get up to investigate. I'd have to wait until mid-morning when my parents went to the hospital and hoped nobody would notice the low water level before then.

I catapulted myself up and over the side of the pool. But before I cleared the pool, my foot banged against the outside metal frame. I cried out in pain, then glanced up to my parents' window. All was calm. I made a run for the kitchen door.

My pajamas— I left them on the grass near the cabana. Shit! I stepped into the flower bed that ran along the side of the house. With my back against the clapboard, I inched my way down the flower bed, passing under my parents' window to the cabana. Then I slowly crawled onto the grass and snatched up the pajamas. I craned my head around and checked my parents' window. My father was standing there. He looked straight down at the pool, then to the left and the right. I crouched in the merciful shadow of the cabana's roof. If he saw me, he'd be down in the kitchen in a flash. Did I leave the door open?

I stayed there another five minutes. The birds were now in a full chattering frenzy as the sky bleached out. I peeked up at my parents' window again. My father was gone. I stepped into my pajamas and crept back into the house and up the stairs like a slinking cat.

The passage in the pool was the way out. But how would I Alice-in-Wonderland my way down that narrow swirling hole? Like it or not, I had to go. If I didn't, Audrey might die. From the safety of my bed, I allowed the sadness to wash over me. After a good cry, I was worn out. Lulled by the calls of a mourning dove, I dozed.

CHAPTER TEN

I awoke to the familiar, mellow whine of a lawn mower. The room was sunny and hot, which meant it was near noon. My mother hadn't roused me. She never let us kids sleep past 9 in the summer. I kicked away the damp sheet that had gotten twisted around my legs. Audrey was being transferred to Deborah Hospital for her heart catheterization today. My parents had probably left early to accompany her.

I shuffled down the hall to the bathroom. A faint smell of cigarettes wafted in from the window above the tub. The lawn mower was nearer. It suddenly sputtered and stopped. I climbed into the tub and peered out the window. My father, cigarette clamped between his teeth, bent down and inspected the dent in the pool's metal wall. Crap. Why wasn't he at the hospital? He ran his hand over the indentation and then tried to pop it back out with his fist. The pool made a tinny groan, but the dent remained. He took off his dirty, white ball cap, smoothed down his comb-over, and then slapped his cap back on.

My father stood back up and put the cigarette back between his fingers. He peered over the side of the pool. "GODDAMMIT!" he shouted. He flicked his cigarette into the grass and squished it with his sneaker. I could tell from the bathroom window too; the water level had gone down— a lot. I thought I put the pool plug in securely.

My father had built a narrow wooden boardwalk that curved around the pool's perimeter. When water splashed out of the pool, the boardwalk prevented muddy feet and grass from getting into the water. I watched him lift one of the boardwalk sections. The ground was saturated. After replacing the boardwalk, he got the ladder and plunged it into the pool. He took off his sneakers, trudged up the ladder in his tee shirt and shorts, and waded to the middle of the pool. My father must have sensed someone was watching him because he shot a glance up to the bathroom window. It was too late for me to duck, so I called down to him. "What're you doing, Dad?"

With his weight on one foot, he stood on the pool plug, forcing it deeper into the bottom of the pool. "The pool's leaking. And there's a big dent on the side. Do you know anything about that?"

"No."

My father climbed out of the pool and grabbed a towel from the cabana. He stood under the window and dried off. Then he cocked his head up. "I'm not accusing you, Honey. I saw you in the hall last night, and then I thought I heard a noise outside. What were you doing up?" He fixed his eyes on me and waited.

"I got hungry. I didn't like the soup Mrs. McGill made," I said, returning his stare. Plausible excuse.

He put his hands on his hips. "Did you go outside?"

"No way."

He studied me a minute longer before turning his attention back to the lawn mower. So I asked, "Aren't you going to the hospital?"

"We're already back, Sleepy Head. Your mother went to the grocery store."

"Is Audrey okay?"

"Lemme finish the lawn, and when your mother comes home, we'll talk to you kids." Before I could respond, he yanked on the lawn mower's pull cord and steered the mower to the patch of grass behind the pool.

He didn't hear me scream, "Tell me now!"

* * *

When my mother came home from the A & P and had put away the groceries, Kiel and I were directed to the living room couch. My parents stood before us, lit cigarettes, taking long drags, and then exhaled streams of smoke like locomotives. Once comfortably nicotined, they bookended us on the couch.

My mother stared at the crystal cigarette box on the coffee table, her cue that she wanted my father to do the talking. He cleared his throat, then began. "So, you guys know that Audrey was transferred to Deborah Hospital for her heart catheterization." My mother moved the cigarette box from the middle of the coffee table to one end, where she squared it up with the corner of the table.

Kiel sat up straight. "Did she go in an ambulance?"

My mother didn't wait for my father to respond. "Yes, she did, Kiel. She had her test this morning. Now we just have to wait for the results."

"When will we know?" I said.

"In a few days, maybe a week," my mother said. "The good news is that Audrey will be coming home tomorrow."

Relieved of his duty to carry the conversation, my father settled in on the couch. I wanted to reach over and put my arm around his shoulder, tell him that everything was going to be okay, but that would have been too grownup, so I just took his rough, freckled hand in mine. My mother told us that Audrey would need to rest, no running or swimming in the pool. Kiel asked if she got any shots.

The good news wasn't good enough to stop the hammering in my chest or stop the guilt from seeping into my gut. I had to fix this. If Audrey wasn't supposed to exert herself, that meant her doctors were taking extra precautions or, worse, suspected her heart was damaged. Things had gone too far. And it was all my fault. I had to get out of here and soon, like before the results of the catheterization. I worried that if the results were on paper, like a tattoo, it would brand Audrey forever.

"Does that mean we don't have to move?" Kiel asked.

My mother stood up and put the cigarette box back in the middle of the table. My father opened his mouth to speak, but my mother interjected, "Let's just see what happens." My mother headed to the kitchen. I guess we were done here.

"Can we go in the pool?" Kiel asked.

My father stood up too. "The pool's leaking. The drain plug doesn't want to stay put, and there's a dent on the side."

My mother turned around. "What? When did that happen?"

"I don't know. Probably during the night. Some hoodlums must have snuck into the pool."

"Maybe we should just take it down, Joe. It's getting old. It was leaking last year too."

I shot a look at my mother."Noooo!"

"What do you mean, no? You kids are always in someone else's pool."

"Can't we just keep it till the end of the summer? I'll keep it filled," I pleaded.

She had a point, though. Each Memorial Day, pools sprouted in yards all over the neighborhood. Pool-hopping was a thing and an excellent way to avoid doing chores. However, our pool was the only one with a swirling blue exit portal.

My father tousled my hair. "I'll tell you what. You fill it today, but if it starts leaking again, it's got to come down. We can't have water seeping into the basement."

"Okay, Dad."

But it wasn't okay. I was running out of time. I had one shot, one shot to swim my way back home.

* * *

I grabbed the hose and flung it over the side of the pool. Kiel watched me from the picnic table. "How long is this going to take?" he asked.

"I don't know, maybe a couple of hours. Why?"

"Nuts. I wanted to cool off before Albert's birthday party. You weren't invited. Albert thinks you're a weirdo."

I turned on the outside faucet. "I really don't care, Kiel." And I didn't. If I were Albert, I would have thought the same about myself.

"The whole neighborhood will be there."

"Is Eve going?"

"Yup."

I needed to talk to her. "What time is the party?"

"Now. Hey, where ya going?"

I passed through the backyard gate and headed up the street to Albert's house. Eve was walking up his driveway when I cupped my hands around my mouth and called to her as loud as I could.

Eve turned and stared at me. I motioned for her to come toward me. She stood for a moment, and then my faithful friend trotted down to the sidewalk.

"I'm sorry I didn't say anything about the party, Renee. I didn't want to hurt your feelings."

"Don't worry about it. That's not why I'm here. I need to talk to you like right now."

Eve looked up the driveway and then back at me. "Okay."

We headed back to my house. I cleared my throat. "You believed me about the force field, right?"

"Yeah."

"And you believed me when I told you about Missy communicating through the 8-Ball."

"Yes, so?"

"Well, I found something last night."

I told Eve about the swirling blue hole in the pool. This time she didn't laugh at me. She stopped abruptly on the sidewalk and turned to me. "I gotta see this."

"You will. It's all connected, Eve. It's all connected to me."

Eve put her hands on her hips. "What do you mean?"

"What I mean is there's something I haven't told you."

Eve clasped my wrist. "Like what?"

When we got back to my yard, I steered her into the cabana and closed the door. The sun illuminated the green corrugated plastic roof, casting an eerie glow on us. I pointed to the built-in bench that ran along the plywood wall. "Sit."

Eve pushed over a couple of squirt guns and goggles and sat. "What else do you wanna tell me?"

"Listen to me very carefully, Eve." I paced back and forth in the small space. I wasn't sure how to tell an eleven-year-old that I was really an adult who had landed back in her childhood.

"Just spit it out."

So I did. "This will sound crazy, but I don't belong here, here, in this place."

"You don't belong in Colonia?"

"I love it here, but no, Eve. Not now. You watch *The Twilight Zone*, right?"

"Yeah," Eve said slowly, eyeing me.

"Through some miracle or maybe a curse, I landed back in time. Maybe I died. I don't know, but I grew up, Eve. I'm not a kid."

Eve brought her knees up to her chest and circled her arms around her legs. "Oh, come on, Renee. That's crazy."

"I know, but it's the truth."

"I think you're cracking up."

"Well, maybe I am, but you'd be too if this stuff happened to you."

"Did Missy say this through the 8-Ball?"

"No, Eve. I didn't even know about Missy until Albert hypnotized me."

"I don't know, Renee. Maybe you should stop playing with that 8-Ball. It's giving you the heebie-jeebies." Eve hugged her knees and stared off. Then met my eyes. "So why are you telling me all this now?"

"Because I need your help."

"So, are you trying to tell me you're a ghost?" Eve said with a grin.

"I don't think so. Do you think I am?"

"No." Eve took a handful of her hair and twisted it around her finger. "So, how did you get here, then?"

"That's the thing. I only have a vague recollection of a water tunnel and then popping up in the pool."

"A water tunnel?" Eve sat up straight and stretched her legs out. "How come you didn't drown?"

"I don't know."

"And you say you're from the future, right?"

"Yeah."

"Prove it."

"I will in a minute." I told Eve about Audrey's heart condition, the swirling hole, and the pool leak. "I have to go back, Eve, and I think that weird hole in the pool is the way out. I have to go through it before my father takes the pool down. But there's a couple of problems."

"Yeah, I'll say."

"The suction sawming from the hole is weak; it sucked down a worm, but I'm too heavy."

"And what's the other problem?"

"It's too small."

"Show me that blue hole thing."

There were a couple of bathing suits drying on nails in the cabana. We both stripped down and put them on. I checked the house. My mother was on the phone, and my father was watching a ball game in the living room. I snuck Eve out of the cabana, and we slithered up the pool ladder and into the pool.

"Now, when I pull the plug, look real quick, Eve."

"Okay."

We took big gulps of air and then lowered ourselves under. Eve hovered above the pool plug, then gave me a nod. I yanked on the plug.

Immediately, the swirling blue hole came into view. Eve made a watery gasp and shot me a surprised look. I nodded. Then I waved my hand over the hole. Eve watched as the hole drew my hand towards it. When it was clear that the suction was too weak to suck my hand in, she shoved my hand away and then tried it herself. She shook her head back and forth in amazement.

I was running out of air. I motioned with my thumb that we had to surface. She nodded and watched me jam the plug back in.

"See?" I said when we surfaced.

Eve slicked back her dripping hair. "That's out a sight."

"Now, do you believe me?"

"Sort of, but how the heck would you get through it?"

"We would need to generate a lot more power to widen the hole and swirl me down it. And I think I know how."

"We?"

"Not just you, Eve. I mean the whole neighborhood."

Eve said it before I did, "You want us to do a whirlpool?"

"Yup."

"When?"

"Tomorrow. When my parents go pick up Audrey. You come over as soon as you see them leave in the station wagon. Okay?"

"Okay." Eve climbed up the ladder. "I better get going, now. Albert will be hurt if I don't show up at his party. I'll tell everyone about the whirlpool."

"No, not yet. I want them to think it's a spur-of-the-moment thing. Also, the neighbors have been calling the house asking about Audrey. If one of the adults gets wind of this massive whirlpool, it might get back to my parents. At least if a parent calls and tattles tomorrow morning, my parents won't be home to get the call."

"But how would you get everyone rounded up in a hurry?" Eve said as we headed back to the cabana to change.

"I was going to ask JP to spread the word tomorrow morning when he makes his cigarette and newspaper deliveries."

"Groovy."

"Well, almost. I still have to deal with Kiel." In a raspy voice I said, "I'll have to give him an offer that he can't refuse."

"What?"

"Never mind."

"You're cracked in the head," Eve chuckled as she buttoned up her blouse. "Renee?"

"What?"

"You were gonna tell me something that happened in the future."

I pushed down the urge to blurt out that JP would die in an automobile accident. If I intervened now, I feared that someone else would pay the price. What if it was Audrey? Besides, I didn't know when or where the accident took place. "Let me think. Okay, it's 1966, right?"

"Yeah?"

"So, the Beatles are going to break up in 1970."

"That's impossible."

"No, really. They are."

Eve flung a towel at me. "Jesus, Renee. Why did you have to tell me that?"

"I don't know. It's just the first thing that popped into my head. Listen. Try to sneak into their concert at Shea Stadium next month. It'll be their last one there."

"DAMN!" Eve shouted as she slammed the cabana door.

* * *

After Eve left, I lingered in the cabana, folding and refolding the musty towels. I had burdened a kid with my surreal predicament, yet I didn't have the guts to bring up her brutish father. I unfolded the towels and hung them up on a couple of nails that jutted out from the back wall of the cabana. Oh hell! I flung open the cabana door. Eve was halfway up the street when I waved at her to come back. "EVE, THERE'S SOMETHING ELSE I NEED TO TALK TO YOU ABOUT," I shouted.

"CALL ME TONIGHT," she shouted back.

* * *

That evening, I watched *Dr. Kildare* on TV. When my parents began dozing on the couch, I slipped into the kitchen and called Eve. She picked up on the first ring. "Hello?"

"Eve, it's me," I whispered.

"Hey, you aren't going to believe what happened at Albert's party. Paddy McGill ate three pieces of birthday cake and then threw up in Albert's backyard and then—"

"Listen, Eve," I interrupted. "I need to ask you something."

"Okay. What?"

"It's about your father."

She exhaled a long sigh. "What about him?"

"I'm a little concerned about you being in the house with your father. You're developing, Eve. Soon you'll have your period. Your father has all those girly magazines."

"So."

"Does he look at you funny?"

"No."

"What about comments? I mean, does he say anything about your appearance or make jokes?"

"No, Renee. Is that why you called me?"

"I'm just a little concerned, Eve."

"Well, don't be. I'm fine."

"Okay, okay, Eve. It's just that when I was vacuuming your room, I noticed your underwear drawer was open a little. So I took a peek in-"

Eve interrupted. "You looked in my underwear drawer?"

"I know what a neat freak you are, but this one drawer looked like someone had gone through it. I was just curious. That's all."

"Did you take anything?"

"No, why?"

"Because my mother's handkerchief is missing," she huffed.

"From your underwear drawer?"

"That's where it's always been. I think my mother put it there before she...before she...left."

"Maybe your father took it."

"My father doesn't look at me funny, and he doesn't go into my underwear drawer. Geesh! Besides, he was so mad about my mother leaving that he threw out all her clothes. He doesn't even know about the handkerchief."

"When did your mother leave? I forgot."

"When I was five."

"And she never tried to contact you?"

Eve went quiet. When she spoke again, her voice cracked. "My father said she didn't want me."

"And you believed him?" Eve sighed again but didn't speak. I continued, "Eve, this just doesn't add up. Why would she leave you a keepsake if she didn't want you?"

"I don't know, Renee."

"What about the wedding picture behind your father's headboard?"

"I told you not to go in there."

"Eve, I was worried about you."

"Well, don't. I'm fine. And I know about the wedding picture. Sometimes, late at night, I hear him talking to her."

"What does he say?"

"I don't know. He just sort of mumbles and cries a little. Hey, listen; I gotta go. I'll see you tomorrow, okay?"

Cries? Mr. Caruso didn't seem like the crying type. "Hey Eve?" But Eve had hung up before I could tell her that I would find out what I could about her mother's disappearance. That man gave me the creeps.

* * *

The next morning I woke up anxious. Today would be the last day in this magical place, and I was petrified. If the massive whirlpool didn't swirl me back to the twenty-first century, I'd remain here, held hostage for my sins by the force field on the Garden State Parkway, knowing that I had caused Audrey's heart condition.

My mother had called up to tell me not to leave the orange juice out on the table, and then they left. I had been too distracted to go downstairs to give my parents one last hug before they headed out to bring Audrey home. I would never see them alive again. I fought back an avalanche of tears as I climbed into my bathing suit.

I made a couple of waffles while I waited for Eve to come over. From the kitchen window, I watched a cardinal flutter above a branch. What would become of this world? Would it fold itself in like a pop-up storybook and then dissolve? What if it didn't? The real eleven-year-old Renee would be left in the wake of my mess, unable to remember or comprehend the events of the last several days. Maybe she/I would go mad. It was clear; I hadn't thought this all the way through.

The coffee pot had already been washed and was air drying upside down on the dish rack. Crap, I could really use a cup this morning. I spotted JP about to round the corner onto Caton Avenue. I slid into my flip-flops and met him in the DeLaune's driveway. After dropping a few cigarette packs into their milk box, he hopped on his bike. He hung on his handlebars while I explained what I wanted him to do. "So, how many kids do you want me to round up?"

"At least twenty."

"That many? Your pool isn't that big."

"Yeah, but some of them might not show up."

"Are you kidding? Not when I tell them you want a fast-moving whirlpool and your parents aren't home. They'll show up. Besides, it's already pretty hot out."

"Okay, I'll be waiting in the backyard. Oh, and tell the kids, I'll serve them waffles when we're done."

"Your mom got that many?"

"Yeah. They were on sale at the A & P. She stocked the downstairs freezer."

"You're coming too, right, JP?"

"Wouldn't miss it," he said, straitening up. He wheeled around me. "See you later, alligator."

But I wouldn't see him after this day. Should I tell him now about some accident that I had no idea when? Haven't I wiggled the universe enough, though? What if someone else dies in his place? The waffles churned in my stomach.

* * *

When I returned home, Kiel was tying his sneakers at the kitchen table. "Where'd YOU go?" he said.

"I was talking to JP. I heard you put on a great magic show at Albert's birthday party."

"It wasn't bad."

"JP said everyone wants to come over and see the tricks again."

"Really? I messed up a couple of the card tricks."

"No, you did great. In fact, Mrs. McGill wants to hire you for her next dinner party."

More lies.

"Anyway, I told JP to tell everyone to come over, Kiel."

"Now? Mom doesn't want kids in the house when she's not home."

"They'll be in the backyard. You can do your tricks right at the picnic table."

Kiel looked befuddled. "Well, I guess that would be alright." He stood up. "I'd better go practice."

"Oh, and I told them they could cool off in the pool first."

"You know we're not allowed in the pool without Mom or Dad home."

"I won't tell if you don't."

Kiel nodded and then took the stairs two at a time up to his bedroom. I heard the backyard gate open. Good. It's about time Eve showed up.

But it wasn't Eve; it was a set of shy twin sisters who lived on Cameo Place. They sat nervously on the hammock while we waited for the rest of the whirlpoolers to arrive. Within minutes, kids flip-flopped through the gate. Some wore duck floats around their waists. They sat at the picnic table or stretched out on the grass. Paddy McGill sat at the top of the pool ladder. Each time the gate opened, I expected to see Eve with her confident stride in her polka dot bathing suit.

When JP herded the last of the kids into the backyard, I asked him if he had seen her.

"Nope. I rang her doorbell. The house was all dark. I don't think anyone's home."

"She's home. I'll go call her. She wouldn't want to miss the whirlpool." I rushed into the kitchen and dialed Eve's number. I let it ring for a long time. Maybe her father was on the warpath again, and she was up late cleaning. She probably overslept. When I went back outside, she wasn't in the yard. I thought about going to the back of her house and yelling up to her bedroom window.

One of the twins ran up to me. "We're hot. Can we go in the pool now?"

"Sure sure," I said, turning my attention back to Eve's house. The living room curtains were drawn. Mr. Caruso's car was gone. Maybe he dragged her to the A & P.

The aluminum pool ladder creaked. Seeing the twins climb up, signaled to the others that it was time. The big kids rushed the ladder. They stood on every rung, waiting for their turn to enter the pool. The ladder wobbled under their weight.

"HEY, HEY, ONE AT A TIME ON THE LADDER!" I shouted. I took one last forlorn look at Eve's house.

The big kids took their spots along the pool's perimeter and began splashing each other. I helped the younger kids up the ladder, then followed, stopping at the top of the ladder. I counted twenty kids bobbing up and down in the water. JP was right; this was a lot of kids for an eighteen-foot diameter pool. Well, it should make for a hell of a whirlpool. "IS EVERYBODY READY?" I shouted like a Barnum and Bailey's ringmaster.

The older kids stopped splashing and yelled back that they were. Was I ready? Ready to leave all this behind? I was afraid. And why wasn't Eve here to see me off, give me a few words of encouragement, say goodbye?

Everyone waded around the pool, plowing through the water. The younger kids bobbed along in their floats or were pushed ahead by older siblings. I waded to the middle of the pool and stood on top of the pool plug.

After the procession had passed the ladder a few times, the water began to churn. I ignored the kicks from scissoring feet that passed by me. Before long, the force of the current began to lift the ladder a few inches off the bottom of the pool. This is usually when a parent would notice and holler at us to "cut it out." JP helped me lift the ladder up and out of the pool. This produced a few hoots and encouraged the kids to move even faster.

JP circled me. "Why aren't you doing the whirlpool?"

"I have to stand on the plug, so it won't pop open."

"Do you want me to stand on it for a while?"

"No, that's okay."

"Well, alright, but you look like you're having trouble keeping your balance. If you get tired, just let me know," JP said as he swam off to join the others.

The water began sloshing over the walls of the pool. A few kids stopped pumping and surfed along with the current. They were getting tired. Some were panting.

"KEEP GOING JUST A LITTLE MORE!" I shouted.

I couldn't wait for Eve any longer. It was time. I took one last look toward the backyard gate. I had burdened Eve with my secret. A secret that would sully her view of the universe forever. "Oh Eve, I wish you were here," I whispered. Then I dove down through the tangle of legs. The swirling water spun me around and around. I plucked open the pool plug and curled myself into a ball. The blue hole gapped open and widened out. I tested the suction with my hand; it was much stronger than before. It just needed to expand a little wider to get my shoulders through. I grabbed the edges of the hole and stretched, surprised that the opening expanded so easily. Then I closed my eyes, stuck my head and shoulders in, and waited to be sucked deep into the hole.

When I opened my eyes, my head and torso were in a beautiful blue underwater tunnel. The water was warm. I knew this place. I propelled myself forward. Behind me, the swirling blue hole closed up. I fought off an urge to turn back. Swallow your fear. The tunnel stretched out about thirty feet before curving around a bend. Shadows flickered off the walls of the bend. I heard echoes, and an urgent voice called my name. Another voice murmured something I couldn't decipher.

I swam toward the bend. I heard a muffled groaning sound coming from behind me. There was a pop. The water tunnel began collapsing around me. A strong current pulled me back toward the pool. I struggled against the current, swimming hard, but the current was stronger. It pulled me back through the mouth of the blue hole, where I landed at the bottom of my pool. Then the swirling blue hole shrunk and closed again.

There were muffled screams. Someone kicked me in the head. When I surfaced, a swift rush of water swept me up and propelled me forward. I opened my eyes. I was riding a fast- moving wave of water across the backyard lawn along with a tumbled sea of thrashing arms and legs.

* * *

Most of us were lucky and sailed right through the open gate onto the front lawn. Two older kids got smacked up against the fence. Kids were lying everywhere. Some were crying; others were laughing.

Perhaps it was a miracle that, except for a few sore shoulders and skinned knees, no one was seriously hurt. As I headed to the house to get Band-Aids and ice, my father's station wagon pulled into the driveway. My father bolted from the car. He slipped and sloshed in his black oxfords across the soggy front lawn. When he got to the jumble of kids lying near the gate, he shrieked, "What in hell did you kids do!"

CHAPTER ELEVEN

It didn't take long for the commotion on our front lawn to attract the whole neighborhood. Parents rushed out of their houses and escorted their shaken kids home.

After my mother settled Audrey on the living room couch, she joined my father and the crowd on the front lawn. I snuck inside and sat on the couch next to Audrey. She looked pale and tired. "How ya feeling, Audrey?"

"THEY STUCK A BIG NEEDLE IN MY THIGH. IT HURT."

The front screen door opened and then snapped shut. I heard my mother's sandals clicking on the floorboards. Her fury punctuated each heavy step. She grabbed me by the elbow and roughly yanked me up the stairs to my room. She pushed me onto the bed. Then she wagged a finger in my face, shouting, "You're gonna stay here, young lady, until I decide what to do with you." On her way out, she slammed the door.

I deserved whatever I had coming to me, but no amount of punishment could wipe away the anguish I felt. Not only had I caused Audrey's heart condition, I had also put the neighborhood kids in danger. And for what? I was still trapped here.

And where was Eve? She and her father were the only two people who didn't come out of their house. JP said no one was home. Where were they then? My room was at the far corner of the house. I got up off the bed and looked out the window. Eve's house was barely visible. I jimmied the screen until it popped out. I dragged the desk chair over to the window and leaned out. Now I could see Eve's driveway. Her father's car was there. She's home! She would be heading over any minute. But surely my mother would turn her away. I would have to keep watch until Eve walked out to her driveway, and then signal her to come to my window.

I hung out the window until my waist, which was pressed against the window frame, began to get sore. Long afternoon shadows filled the room. The phone rang a few times downstairs. Apparently no message from Eve, though. Or maybe I wasn't allowed messages in captivity. I replaced the screen. Quietly, I opened the bedroom door and peered down to the living room. Audrey was asleep on the couch. The smell of fried Taylor Ham drifted from the kitchen. My stomach growled with anticipation of the Spam-like exquisiteness. I had missed lunch; hopefully, my mother would let me eat supper. I yelled down to the kitchen. "Hey, Mom, can I come out now?"

My mother came to the foot of the stairs. "No, you may not."

"But I'm hungry."

"You should have thought of that before."

"Wonderful," I grumbled as I headed to the bathroom.

From the bathroom window, I could see down Westminster Road. JP was bouncing a basketball in his driveway. He would be making his evening cigarette rounds soon. He could find out what happened to Eve. I watched him shoot and then miss the basketball net attached above his garage door. "JP!" I yelled out the bathroom window. He dribbled and made another shot. The basketball hit the rim and ricocheted off. JP dribbled in a circle, leaped up and shot. The basketball rimmed the basket and fell in. I sucked in my breath and bellowed as loud as I could, "JPEEEEEEE!" Nothing. Presumably wanting to quit on a high note, he picked up his basketball and headed into his garage. Defeated, I headed back to my room.

My mother was waiting at the bottom of the stairs. "Stop hollering out the window, Renee."

"Sorry, Mom."

* * *

When evening came, there was still no knock on the front door or phone call from Eve. I wondered if she was annoyed with me for bringing up the touchy subject of her mother or her father. When my mother brought Audrey up to bed, I asked her if I could call Eve.

"I think Eve called a couple of hours ago. Kiel took the message."

So she did call! She must be so worried about me. "I have to talk to Eve, Mom."

"You can call her back tomorrow."

"What!" I huffed.

My mother glared at me. "You heard me."

I felt the anger rise in my chest, but I was relieved. Eve wasn't mad about my questioning her about her father, or at least she had gotten over it. When my mother went down to the rec room, I ran to the top of the stairs. "Kiel, Kiel, come up here a minute."

My brother took his sweet time getting up from the couch. He stood at the bottom of the stairs. "What?"

"Did Eve call?"

"Yeah."

"What did she say?"

"She said she's not home. Said something about being at an aunt's."

"Who? WHAT AUNT?" I barked.

"I don't know. Stop yelling at me."

"Okay, I'm sorry, Kiel."

Eve never talked about an aunt. There were no relatives on her mother's side. That meant the aunt was the father's sister or some other woman with this dubious honor. It didn't make sense that Eve would take off when I needed her help, though. And it wasn't like her not to tell me. I lowered my voice. "Did you take down the number?"

"Noooo. But I think Eve said she'd try to call you back."

"WHEN?" I was back to shouting.

"I don't know!" Kiel walked away from the staircase. "You're such a crab," he said over his shoulder.

My father came up the stairs holding a tray. I picked up the aroma of fried Taylor Ham on toasted white. The smell of the sausage-like ham sent up a gurgle from my empty stomach.

The grease from the ham had seeped into the center of the bread, producing a golden circle of greasy goodness. Childhood favorites like these are what dreams are made of. Although I was famished, I ate slowly, savoring each salty, chewy bite.

Audrey watched me from her bed. After I had washed down my fine meal with the glass of whole milk, I sat next to her. "Hey, Audrey. Feeling any better?"

"YEAH, A LITTLE. I'M SORRY YOU WERE STUCK IN HERE ALL DAY."

"I'm fine, Audrey. You get some rest. Tomorrow we can play board games if you want."

"I WANNA PLAY *CANDYLAND*," she yawned.

* * *

The next day my recompense continued with house cleaning, which I performed with anxious gusto. Every time the phone rang, I picked up on the first ring. A few neighbors called about Audrey. Then my Uncle Gene called. Before I handed the phone to my mother, he kidded me about watering the lawn. My mother chatted with him in Italian while I swept the kitchen floor. I played five games of *Candyland* and then *Chutes and Ladders* with Audrey until she felt groggy.

Finally, at five o'clock, Eve called. I coiled the phone cord tightly around my shoulders. "Eve, where are you? I've been so worried. Are you alright? How come-"

Eve cut me off. "Renee, stop talking. I don't have much time. I'm calling from a pay phone."

"A pay phone?"

"He knows, Eve."

"Who? Knows what?"

"My father. He heard everything you said about my mother. He was listening on the extension when you called the other night. He got angry. He did steal the handkerchief, Eve. Then he dragged me out of bed in the middle of the night, and we drove for hours on the highway. That's why I wasn't there for the whirlpool."

"Oh my God...Where are you now?"

"I'm somewhere in Pennsylvania. I kept track of the road signs for as long as I could, but then I must have dozed off. I'm on a farm, staying with this old lady. She says she's my aunt, but I don't know her, and she's mean. There are other kids here too. They won't talk to me."

"Jesus, Eve. How long are you going to be there?"

"I don't know. Every time I ask questions, she tells me to shut up."

"We have to get you out of there. Get me the address and phone number."

"She doesn't have a phone. I snuck out when she went into town. I walked down the road and found this phone booth."

"This is all my fault, Eve. I'll tell my parents. They can help. You have to get me an address, though. Try to find some mail."

"Okay, I'll try, but she locks us in our bedrooms at night. Anyway, how are you doing? Yesterday when I called to see if you, you know, went through the blue water hole, Kiel said the pool burst."

"Yup."

Please insert 10 cents for an additional 10 minutes.

Eve's voice sped up. "And then it dawned on me that there may be another way to get you out."

"Eve, don't worry about me." The phone clicked. "Eve, are you still there?"

"Yeah. I don't have any more money. You have to find another portal, Renee. It's possible. I read it in one of my comics. You'll have to sneak into my room. Grab the stack of comics on my desk. Find the time travel tale."

Eve had her own troubles and here she was talking about a portal for me. There was another click and then dead air. "Eve, Eve!" I hung up the phone. My hands were shaking. She seemed to be locked away at some sort of foster home or work farm. And to be taken there during the night was suspicious. She needed my help.

My mother was folding clothes in her bedroom. I sat on the bed and told her that Eve had been whisked away in the middle of the night by her father. "We have to help her, Mom."

"Hmm. That does sound cruel. But Mr. Caruso is her father. What do you expect us to do?"

"Call the police!"

"And say what? Her father kidnapped her and brought her to a farm? Don't be ridiculous, Renee."

"But he took Eve after she started asking questions about her mother." My mother wouldn't look at me. She folded and refolded the same bath towel, so I continued, "First, her mother disappears, and now Eve is taken away. Don't you think that's strange?"

"Her mother didn't just disappear. You're too young to understand these things, Renee."

"No, I'm not. And I know you don't believe she ran away either."

"You don't know what you're talking about."

"I heard you, Mom, at the barbecue. Uncle Gene was there and a bunch of neighbors. You said you didn't think Juanita just up and left."

"What barbecue? I never said that."

I was floored. Why was my mother denying something I so clearly remembered? "Then what happened to her, Mom? Tell me that."

My mother grabbed another bath towel from the laundry basket and began smoothing it down on the bed. "Listen, Renee. Not all marriages are good ones. Mrs. Caruso was unhappy."

"I'm sure she was, Mom, but why would Mr. Caruso get so mad that he banishes Eve to Pennsylvania?"

My mother threw down the towel. "I don't know, Renee. Look, right now, my concern is Audrey."

"But Mom!"

"No more, Renee. You're giving me a headache. Why don't you ask Mr. Caruso for her address? Maybe you two can write to each other. I'm sure she'll be back before school starts in September."

"But what if she's not?"

"That's the end of it, Renee! Here, go put these away," she said, pressing a tower of towels against my chest.

But I knew Eve wouldn't be back. She had vanished that summer back in 1966. The difference was that Fate had just re-calibrated itself this time around. Instead of Eve running off after the barbecue, Eve had been whisked away during the night. And it was all my fault.

"UGH!" I screamed in frustration as I stomped out of my parent's bedroom. There had to be another way to get Eve home. And I wasn't leaving this place until I did.

* * *

So it was up to me to find Eve and spring her from that work farm. But the question was, where was she? I could sneak into her house, rummage around, and maybe find this phony aunt's address or phone number. I grinned. You trained for this. It would be the same as snooping around the house to find where my mother hid the Christmas presents. My brother and I would wait until my mother was out shopping and then tear around the house looking in back of closets, under our parent's bed, and in the crawl space. We always found them. It was a letdown though because it took the excitement out of Christmas morning, but we still did it.

I had watched Eve sneak into her house through her bedroom window for years. Her father would be on the warpath about something, like not having his work shirts ironed or when his supper wasn't on the table when he got home from his shift. He would confine her to her room. And then, when he fell asleep on the couch in front of the TV, Eve would sneak out. It was an easy jump from her bedroom window to the cement patio below. We would run through the woods in the back of her house, down to the creek behind Jordan Road, pretending to be Illya Kuryakin and Napoleon Solo from *The Man From U.N.C.L.E.*, escaping evil captors. When it got late, we would each take a handle of her aluminum trash can, which squatted on a dirt patch next to the patio. We would then carry the trash can across the cement patio and place it under her window. Eve would then scramble on top of the can and hoist herself up and through her bedroom window. Once inside, she would hang out the window and watch me bear hug the trash can back to the dirt patch. After completing this task, she would always whisper, "Mission accomplished, Solo!" and shut the window. I asked her once why the trash can was kept next to the patio instead of on it. "My father doesn't like anything on the patio," was her answer.

Today was different. I would be on my own and with no cover of darkness. I waited until Mr. Caruso pulled out of the driveway to go to work, then hurried across the street.

The shades were all drawn, a painful reminder that Eve was gone. A car drove by. When it rounded the corner onto Caton Avenue, I walked around to the back of the house, following the row of windows. Eve's room was at the far end.

Compared to the scraggly front lawn, the backyard grass was cropped as neatly as a crew cut. And no weeds were poking up between the cement slabs of the patio. The old, dented aluminum garbage can was on the dirt patch next to the patio. The can was nearly empty, so it was easy to roll it myself towards Eve's window. I hopped up on it and stood up slowly, balancing myself as the can rocked in protest.

Eve's usually spotless room was a wreck. Her bed linens were pulled off the bed, and the closet was wide open. Most of her clothes were gone. A white blouse dangled by a shoulder on a wire hanger.

The bureau drawers were open. I put a knee on the window sill and gave the window a good upward shove. It didn't budge. I checked the lock. It wasn't latched. The humidity from the summer's heat must have sealed it shut. With a mighty heave on the second try, the window opened with a squeak, but the force of my efforts knocked the can from under me. The lid popped off and clanged as it hit the patio. A beer bottle rolled out lazily and meandered across the patio. I clung to the windowsill, feeling for the clapboards below the window with my feet. Then I took a deep breath and launched myself into Eve's room, landing on the floor with a thud. Immediately, a sharp pain pierced my knee. "Son of a bitch!" I cried out, rubbing my knee.

When the pain subsided, I hobbled to Eve's bureau. Her underwear drawer was empty, the contents strewn about on the floor with her shorts and pajamas. Even if Eve had to pack in a hurry, she wouldn't have dumped out drawers.

Her desk drawers were open too. The stack of comics that Eve wanted me to take was scattered haphazardly on top.

Strewn on the floor next to the desk were pens and pencils along with the pencil holder we had all made in Mrs. Karkus's fourth-grade class the year before. While most of the girls covered their tin cans with fashion models cut from magazines, Eve covered hers with comic book heroines: Sheena, Queen of the Jungle, Wonder Woman, and Marvel Girl. I tenderly stacked the comics and placed the can back on the desk.

I headed downstairs to the kitchen. The sink was full of dishes with stuck-on food, and the kitchen smelled of garbage. What a slob; he gave up his maid for what? On the counter was a heap of mail. There were no out-of-state return addresses. The slimy kitchen trash barrel contained none either.

In the kitchen junk drawer, I found a dog-eared fake leather phone book. I knew the area codes for New Jersey and New York but not Pennsylvania. I grabbed a pen with a chewed tip. On my wrist, I wrote down every name and phone number that didn't contain a New Jersey or New York area code. There were five numbers with names; all were women.

I returned to Eve's room and sat at her desk. I scanned the comics: *Fantastic Four*, *Journey into Mystery Annual*, *Strange Tales*, and *Evergreen Review*. I thumbed through *The Evergreen Review*, stopping at a story titled "The Adventures of Phoebe Zeit-Geist," about a kidnapped debutante who Nazis later rescued. Really Eve? Next, I picked up a *Marvel Comic* series called *Strange Tales*. On the cover, Eve had circled the cover story: "Billy's Time Machine." I put this one on top of the heap. I didn't put much stock in Eve's whacky theory, but it wasn't any wackier than me landing here.

Since the trash barrel under Eve's window had tipped over, I wasn't going to leap out her window with my sore knee, which had begun to throb. I would have to sneak out the kitchen door and hope no one would see me. I took another look around the ransacked room. Mr. Caruso did this, searching for the handkerchief. Why would he care that his daughter had one keepsake from her mother? The Minnie Mouse clock on Eve's desk said that it was noon. Plenty of time to snoop around some more. With Eve's comics pressed against my chest, I headed down the hall to Mr. Caruso's bedroom.

His bed was unmade, with the linens peeled over the end of the bed onto the floor. I lifted the bedsheets that smelled like dirty hair and peered under the bed; nothing but the same wispy globs of dust and underwear. The nightstand's top drawer was empty except for a crumpled-up Raleigh cigarette pack and a gold butane lighter. The bottom drawer was larger and heavier. Inside were stacks of *Playboy* magazines. Sneering with disgust, I lifted the pile with two fingers and looked underneath for the handkerchief.

There was a sound outside, heavy footsteps on the concrete patio. I pressed myself against the wall and stole a glance out the window. Mr. Caruso. Shit. He knows that I talked to Eve about her mother's disappearance. If he finds me in his house, he'll know I was here to snoop around. He stood with his hands on his hips and peered up at Eve's window and down at the trash can on its side. Did I close her window? I didn't think so. He muttered something, righted the can, slammed on the lid, and then carried the can off the patio. The kitchen door banged open. Floorboards moaned under quick footsteps throughout the first floor. Hide.

I grabbed the comics and slid under Mr. Caruso's bed, which was alongside one wall. I pressed my body against the wall. I tugged at the dirty top sheet until it came loose. Then I covered myself with it. If he looked under, I hoped he would just see the bunched-up top sheet stuffed between the wall and the bed, and not me.

Mr. Caruso bounded up the stairs. He went to Eve's room first. I heard her bed being lifted by its frame and then banged down. Oh, God. He stomped down the hall. Then he was here in his room. I heard him open the closet door, then the tinkle of hangers being shoved to one side.

Footsteps were coming toward the bed. Would he lift a double bed frame or just peer under? I held my breath. There was rustling. Then silence except for the thumping of my heart. He must be looking under the bed.

The footsteps resumed. This time they were coming around the end of the bed towards the wall. Did I completely cover myself? Would he tug on the sheet, discover me and then drag me out?

Mr. Caruso let out a long breath. Then footsteps headed out of the room. I let out a long breath too. He would go back to work soon. I would have to wait him out. When I threw off the sheet, my knee had swelled to the size of a baseball. Wonderful.

* * *

I wasn't bored for the first hour. When my eyes adjusted to the darkness, I opened the "Billy's Time Machine" comic and began reading. Billy, his little sister, and his friends built a make-believe time machine out of a discarded cardboard refrigerator box. They set it down under a tree in Billy's backyard. A big thunderstorm blew in, so the kids huddled in the time machine to wait out the storm. Predictably, the tree was struck by lightning which sent a shock through the ground under the time machine. The kids were knocked unconscious. When they came to, Billy's little sister was gone. All that was left of her was one pink flip-flop. Cute story, Eve, but I'm not going to sit under a tree and get electrocuted. I continued reading. They got Billy's sister back, not by way of the flopped-over, water-logged time machine, but through a portal they had found in an abandoned drainage tunnel. On this page, Eve had circled the word portal in red crayon and wrote the word creek above it. But Eve, I don't remember a drainage tunnel down by the creek.

Occasionally, I heard Mr. Caruso walking about. I heard the flush of a toilet and the opening and closing of the refrigerator, which called attention to my full bladder and empty stomach. By the time I had gone through the rest of the comics, I had realized that Mr. Caruso wasn't returning to work. The stripping sound of a beer can being opened confirmed this. During the second hour, footsteps moved up the stairs. And then I smelled his body odor. Mr. Caruso was back in the bedroom. My heart quickened. I felt light-headed. Don't pass out.

From under the bed, I could see a sliver of the room. Mr. Caruso's heavy black work boots clumped toward me. The boots stood at the bedside motionless. I held my breath. Then the boots lifted off the floor. The bed creaked as the full weight of Mr. Caruso sagged the mattress and box spring, settling inches from my nose. I instinctively turned my head away. He's lying down? Then new sounds: another beer being stripped open, gulping. He was drinking a beer. He was lying on top of me, drinking a beer. My knee spasmed twice as if to say yes.

After several minutes, Mr. Caruso let out a long belch. The bed groaned; then the boots were back on the floor. Finally, he's leaving. I let out another long breath. However, the boots didn't walk themselves out of the room. Instead, they were pulled off. Next, I heard rustling and the tinkling of a belt buckle. Soon blue work pants pooled around the boots, followed by white briefs. Oh boy.

The bed jiggled with his movements. Then the grunting started. The room began to fill with more of his sour perspiration. I wanted to scream. I wanted to bolt from under the bed and run out of there, but I laid there quietly with my hand cupped over my mouth.

When the grunting stopped, there was slow, even breathing. It was now or never. Inch by inch, with the comics held close to my chest, I wormed my way carefully out from under the bed, careful not to knock the hairy leg that dangled over the side. When I had crawled to the doorway, I looked back. Mr. Caruso was sprawled with his legs spread apart. His shriveled uncircumcised penis lay limp on a patch of glistening black pubic hair. Ewww.

Something white on the nightstand caught my eye. It was a dainty, embroidered handkerchief folded neatly on the corner of the nightstand, Juanita's handkerchief! Mr. Caruso must have found it after all. Bastard. I could make it to the nightstand in five easy steps, maybe six. I slowly tiptoed, one step at a time. I swiped the handkerchief. It was clean, unsullied by Mr. Caruso's urgings. Mr. Caruso stirred and mumbled something in his sleep. I stood in a Freeze Tag pose. When his breathing returned to a steady rhythm, I tiptoed out of the room and headed down the stairs.

Passing through the kitchen, I noticed a fresh crop of mail on the kitchen table. I ignored a warning flutter from my bladder and picked up the pile. It was mostly junk mail except for one opened envelope. The return address read Philadelphia, PA; it was empty, though. My heart sped up. I scanned the kitchen for the contents of the envelope. Again

I rummaged through the damp trash. I checked the living room. Nothing.

Footsteps were coming down the stairs. I jammed the envelope and Juanita's handkerchief into my pocket. I pulled on the kitchen doorknob. The door was swollen shut. "Come on, come on," I whispered, yanking on the doorknob.

I smelled him before a heavy hand gripped my shoulder. "No you don't."

I tried to yank myself free, but Mr. Caruso grabbed the collar of my blouse and swung me around. "Let go of me!"

His pants were back on, zipped up to his bare beer gut. "What are you doing here?" he growled.

"Where is Eve?" I yelled back at him.

"None of your business," he said, digging his fingernails into my shoulder. His stale beer breath made me recoil and twist away from him, which made him dig his nails further into my shoulder. I continued to squirm and twist, not noticing that the envelope was unfurling in my pocket until it worked itself out and fluttered to the floor.

"What ya got there?" he said, sneering at me. When I didn't answer, he bent down and scooped up the envelope. In that brief moment, his grip on my shoulder loosened. I gave him a mighty shove with my free hand. He fell backward, letting go of me. His head banged on the floor. I swung my good leg back and kicked him hard in the crotch. The crumpled-up envelope slipped out of his hand. He folded himself into a fetal position, cradling his crotch with both hands, eying me like a wounded whale. "You little bitch!" he screeched.

I calmly snatched up the envelope, gathered the comics, and let myself out the kitchen door. Twitching with adrenalin, I hobbled across the street. "Mission accomplished, Napoleon Solo."

CHAPTER TWELVE

My mother's VW Beetle was gone from the driveway. The garage door was left open, something she never did. This bothered me. Did she leave in a hurry and was distracted? From what?

The cool, damp air of the garage calmed me a bit. I stopped to catch my breath beside my father's old workbench, which stood silently against the back wall of the garage. I absently turned the handle of the vice grip mounted on one corner of the workbench recalling the time after we moved to Massachusetts when my father had held the family cat in the vice to retrieve a chicken bone lodged in the cat's throat. He was so gentle with the cat. The memory made me smile.

In the rec room bathroom, I relieved my full bladder. I took four aspirin from the medicine cabinet and splashed cold water on my face. "You've made a mess of things once again," I said to my 11-year-old reflection in the mirror as I dried off. Mr. Caruso would retaliate. He'll figure out I know where Eve is AND that I swiped the handkerchief. He'll say I broke into his house and stole something near and dear to his heart. Blah, blah, blah. Yet his stealing the only keepsake of Juanita and then whisking Eve away like that was worse. I reached into my pocket and touched the handkerchief. I'll get you back, Eve. And when I do, your mother's handkerchief will be back where it belongs.

Kiel was bounding down the rec room stairs as I hobbled up them. "Where yah been?" he asked.

"I went for a walk. Where did Mom go?"

"She took Audrey back to Deborah hospital."

"Why, what happened?" I barked.

"They got Audrey's catheterization results-."

"What'd it say?" I interrupted.

"I don't know. What's wrong with your knee?"

"What do you mean, you don't know. Didn't you ask?"

"Jeez. Calm down, Renee. Mom didn't say. She just got Audrey in the car and left. Why do you always have to be such a crank?" he said, turning on the TV.

I looked at Kiel for a long moment. Time was running out for Audrey. I had to find this so-called portal before Audrey's catheterization declared heart disease. If I failed, Audrey could wither and die like Tiny Tim in Charles Dickens' *A Christmas Carol*.

There was no time for farewells or pointers for Kiel on navigating the stormy seas of adolescence. "Be brave," was all I could muster before heading back outside.

"I am brave. You be brave," he sassed back.

* * *

Eve's notation on the Billy comic indicated I should go down to the creek. It sounded crazy, but there I was, hobble sprinting across Paddy McGill's backyard to the creek behind Jordan Road.

The brackish-colored water meandered over the smooth rocks wedged into the muddy bottom of the creek. Crayfish streaked between the rocks like commuters veering around shoppers on a city sidewalk.

I pulled off my flip-flops and stepped into the ankle-deep water. I sloshed along the creek until I came to a low cement slab. Because of the lack of rain, the creek bed was nearly dry at this end. I had forgotten about this strange barge of concrete that had squatted there for decades. The platform stood four feet tall and about eight feet long. Etched into the stone was the year 1927. No one knew why it was there. Perhaps it was debris dumped from a construction site. I remembered trying to catch crayfish near here. Eve would sit on top of the structure, legs dangling, and warn me when I was about to step on a snapping turtle.

I walked around the structure, looking for an opening. On the back side was a cave-like crevice under the structure formed by erosion. It was just big enough for me to crawl in. So this was Eve's idea of a portal?

I laid on my stomach and muttered some mumbo jumbo, crossed myself twice, then clicked my two muddy heels together. This was silly. When a mosquito hovered over my arm, ready to dive bomb, I crawled out and hefted myself on top of the structure.

From this vantage point, I could hear the whisper of traffic from the Garden State Parkway. The force field. I had forgotten how it hung across the overpass like an iron curtain. There had been muffled voices coming from the other side. It had beeped. Eve had heard it too. Was that the portal? I was so focused on the pool exit that I hadn't considered the force field as an escape route.

I hobbled back through the woods behind Westminster Road. I'd be stuck at this end of Colonia forever if I couldn't break through the force field. I headed toward the overpass and then stopped. Something else gnawed at me again. After I vaporized and time re-aligned itself, what would happen to the real me, the one who lived in this slice of time? I had pushed away the conundrum several times, but now it slithered through me like an eel, burrowing itself deep within me. Would she go mad with confusion and paranoia, or would she awake and shake it off as just a crazy dream? Perhaps it didn't matter. Perhaps the fabric of this place would unravel like an old knit sweater. What if it didn't? I took long gulps at the playground fountain. The water tasted as pure as any trendy bottled water. What if I left instructions before I broke through the force field? There was the diary, my diary. It was sitting right there in the top drawer of the desk all this time. I had flipped through it when I was detained in my room. I could explain things, leave instructions. Deborah Hospital was at least an hour away, or did it just seem like that when I was a kid? It was late in the day. Surely my mother would get caught in rush-hour traffic. There was still time. But what would I say that wouldn't scare the bejesus out of an eleven-year-old? I pondered this as I turned around and headed home.

* * *

I ignored Kiel's "How'd you get so filthy?" as I made my way back through the rec room and up to my bedroom. I retrieved Juanita's handkerchief from my pocket and then changed out of my soiled clothes.

The last diary entry was dated July 5, 1966, the day before I landed here. In that entry, in my best school penmanship, I had written about the barbecue the day before. I had troubled over Eve; how she took off running back to her house after overhearing my mother tell everyone that she didn't think Juanita just up and left.

I stared at the blank July 6 page. I had to fill the next few pages with something plausible to explain the events of the last several days. And I had to keep it light, so I began.

Dear Diary, I had the craziest dream...

* * *

When I put the pen down, I had filled up the rest of July. In my crazy dream pretense, I included Albert hypnotizing me. When it came to Audrey, I paused and mindlessly began doodling hearts on the page instead. Finally, I wrote: *In my dream, Audrey was a little tired. I know it's just a dream, but I'll keep a close eye on her anyway.*

I absently folded and refolded Juanita's handkerchief. I had no words. Audrey's Barbie alarm clock warned that it was 4:15. My mother's VW had not yet sputtered up the street. "Oh hell," I said shutting the diary.

From the middle drawer, I grabbed a sheet of loose-leaf paper. Scrunched up in the back of the drawer, I found a few dog-eared envelopes and stamps left over from my pen pal writing phase. I began my letter with *To Whom this may concern.* I wrote that Eve was held captive at a work farm. I included the address from the envelope I had swiped from Eve's kitchen. I pleaded for an investigation, stating that the farm was violating child labor laws. I had no idea if that was true, but I hoped that at the very least, it would get someone's attention.

When I was done, I stuffed the letter into an envelope. I was about to address it to the Colonia Police department, but a letter obviously penned by a child would probably end up in the trash as just a prank from a bored neighborhood kid. Instead, I addressed it to the one person who'd be my best shot: my mother.

* * *

As I limped down Westminster Road to the corner mailbox, the sky grew dark, with thick angry clouds closing in. A damp wind whipped American flags hanging from porches and flower pots. Rain began to spit. I paused for a moment before dropping the letter into the blue mailbox. My heart pulsated up to my jaw. I was flirting with Fate, Eve's fate once again. I took a deep breath and then headed to the Garden State Parkway overpass to confront my nemesis for the last time. This time I would pass through it or die trying.

By the time I had rounded the corner near School 17, the fog had rolled in, and the rain was coming down in sheets. I was cold. A clap of thunder rumbled in the distance. I had hoped the school would be open for Summer School or meetings like it had been on that first day when the teachers burst through the door. I tried the front door. It was locked and no lights were on. I stood in the doorway, allowing myself a few moments of self-pity while I waited for the storm to pass. If I had a cell phone, I'd call for an Uber to whisk me back home.

The sky was clearing over St. John Vianney church. When the rain petered to a drizzle, I resumed my mission. The fog had not cleared, however; instead, it thickened as I walked along the usually busy Inman Avenue. Today it was very quiet; no cars whizzed by, and no dogs barked at me from front yards. I still couldn't hear cars when I approached the Garden State Parkway overpass. Perhaps there was a car crash below, and all traffic had stopped. I would hear sirens soon, I reasoned.

And then I did hear something, a cough? It came from behind me, cloaked in the fog. Someone was on the sidewalk about one house away. I whirled around, waiting for the person to show themselves. The sidewalk was empty.

I continued walking. When I got to the overpass, I stuck my hands out, feeling for the force field. I walked slowly, step by step. Where is the bloody thing? I took another step. Then I stopped and peered over the guard rail. No cars zipped below on the Garden State Parkway. And no cars were coming over the overpass either. It was rush hour. Where was everyone? I stood in the middle of the street, listening for a car to bump onto the overpass. Silence; I started to feel dizzy. I took a couple of deep, slow breaths and continued across.

When I had reached the middle of the overpass, I still hadn't encountered the force field. My heart began to race. I stole a glance behind me, hoping whoever had coughed would emerge from the fog and tell me where the force field had gone. "HELLO,

HELLO, HELLO!" I shouted into the fog. No response. Maybe I imagined someone there.

When I had crossed to the other side of the overpass and stepped on the pavement, I broke into a cold sweat. The force field was gone. A few days ago, I would have been elated knowing that my nemesis had disappeared, but now a hopeless doom closed in on me. The force field was supposed to be my portal home. Now what? I sat on the guard rail and buried my face in my hands. There was nothing left to do but head back to my house. If I were alone in this world, I would take refuge there.

I stopped at the playground water fountain again, this time to let the cool water flow over my head and neck. There was a shuffling sound behind me like someone was walking with ill-fitting clod-hoppers. I jerked my head up, scraping the scaly metal faucet on my cheek. "Are you following me? SHOW YOURSELF!" I shouted into the fog. No response. You're alone, idiot. Alone and losing your mind. A wave of nausea percolated in my stomach. I was left with an empty world, void of people, void of the flurry of life. I was alone. I knelt on the ground and vomited.

CHAPTER THIRTEEN

I needed to get home; I'd be safe there. I hurried the rest of the way home, occasionally stopping to listen for footsteps. Someone was back there in the fog following me, stopping when I did.

In front of me, I could see the outline of my house. My mother's VW was in the driveway! For a moment, I felt relieved that I was not alone. Then came the realization that I had failed. Audrey's catheterization would show a heart condition because I hadn't slipped through the force field in time to save her. I ran through the front door. "Mom, Mom!" I called.

In the kitchen, a cigarette rimmed with tangerine lipstick lay smoldering in the beanbag ashtray. "Mom?" I bounded up the stairs. I called out to each family member and checked all the bedrooms and bathrooms; all empty.

I scrambled down the rec room stairs. The TV was on and tuned to *Let's Make a Deal*, but there was no sound. It appeared as though every room was a real-life version of a Fanch Ledan painting.

The adult Kiel loved the artist because his interior paintings depicted the evidence of people yet the rooms were empty of humanity as if the inhabitants were suddenly called away. "What the hell?" I took deep, slow breaths to calm myself. Why is this happening and why now?

I returned to my bedroom. *Go Home* was the last response from Missy. I picked up the Magic 8-Ball. It was wet. My stomach tightened. Running across the glass bottom window was a long crack. Shit!

"Missy, what happened?" I gave the ball a delicate shimmy. Only a feeble puddle of gray liquid remained under the crack.

I waited. "Come on, come on!" I stared at the glass window, willing a message to appear. When it didn't, I crumpled to the floor, gently rolling the Magic 8-Ball in my palm, watching the last of the milky gray liquid ooze from its cracked skull. Now I was truly alone, my punishment for not saving Audrey. The tears came easily.

CHAPTER FOURTEEN

The daytime fog turned into nighttime fog. I sat at the kitchen table and ate my mother's cold fried chicken, thankful that at least the food was real; I wondered for how long. After dinner, I moved through the rooms, turning on lights. How strange to have electricity too. Somewhere there had to be people running the power plants. Down in the rec room, the same episode of *Let's Make a Deal* was on TV. Monty Hall ceremoniously slid open door number one to reveal a brand new 1966 Mustang Convertible.

I checked the standing freezer in the laundry room. It was stocked with waffles, roasts, frozen dinners, and a few cartons of A & P brand ice cream. I grabbed the Neapolitan ice cream. I'd start on the strawberry and then work my way to the chocolate. I headed up the stairs for a spoon. There was that weird clomping, shuffling sound again. It was coming from one of the bedrooms. Good, finally someone came home. "Hello?" I called out. I put the carton of ice cream down on the kitchen table and cocked my head to listen. There it was again. This time the steps were quicker but muffled as if someone was running along the carpeted, upstairs hallway. "Hey Kiel, want some ice cream?" I called out.

When I didn't hear his footsteps, I tiptoed to the foot of the stairs. I froze. On the landing, standing in the dim light, was a hazy figure of a small girl in white cotton pajamas. She stared at me with wide, terrified eyes hidden behind disheveled hair. She glanced toward my bedroom, then back at me like a trapped animal. Holy shit! I felt around for the light switch next to the stairs, but she had darted into my bedroom before I could switch on the light. Where did she come from? "Hey, wait! Who are you?" I called, running up the stairs.

I scanned my bedroom, checked the closet. From under the bed, I heard a whimper. I got down on my hands and knees and lifted the bed covers. The little girl was huddled in a ball near the foot of the bed. Although her face was half-hidden under her hair, I knew from the depth of my soul who she was. As calmly as I could while my heart battered my chest, I whispered, "Come on out. I won't hurt you." Her terror-stricken eyes filled with tears. I reached out my hand, but she scooted further away from me. "I know you're scared. I'm scared too."

She turned her face away from me. It would have been easy to walk around to the other side of the bed and pull her out, but why frighten her even more? I stood up. "I'm going downstairs. I'll be in the kitchen. I have ice cream if you want some."

In a distracted shock, I took two bowls from the cupboard, grabbed the ice cream scoop and a couple of spoons. I absently squeezed the carton of ice cream. It was beginning to soften. What was she doing here? After a few minutes, I heard clomping coming down the stairs.

Standing before me, in the kitchen doorway, was a replica of myself, only younger. How could this be? Time seemed to be overlapping itself again. Why? She had the freckles, the wavy red hair frizzled by a Toni home permanent my mother had frequently dripped on my head. On her feet, I recognized the scuffed-up white rubber rain boots I had begged my mother to buy because they looked like go-go boots. But there was something unfamiliar about this replica that I just couldn't put my finger on. "I have strawberry," I said, surprised that my voice sounded so jittery. "Your favorite!"

She watched me plop a mushy scoop of strawberry ice cream into a bowl. From the corner of my eye, I saw her shift from one foot to the other. Gone was the frightful stare from under the bed. I slid the bowl down to the end of the table. Then I scooped out ice cream for myself. "It's melting," I warned, still not meeting her eyes. The spoon trembled in my hand as I lifted it to my mouth. "It's really goooood," I coaxed.

She coughed. That cough was the same cough I had heard near the Garden State Parkway overpass and at the playground. She had followed me home. A moment later, she clomped her way to the kitchen table and sat in front of the ice cream bowl I had put out for her. Her face was flushed, and I got a whiff of her sweaty, fever hair. Through side-ways glances, I watched her mix the ice cream around in the bowl until it was a soft-serve swirl. She brought a spoonful of ice cream to her mouth. When she swallowed, she winced in pain. I turned toward her. Her cheek was swollen, and there was an egg-shaped lump under her ear. She continued eating her ice cream, wincing with each swallow.

"I know you're sick. You have the mumps, don't you?" I said gently. She didn't look at me. She sat calmly, swinging her legs under the table as she ate. "You have a fever."

After finishing her bowl of ice cream, she clomped her way back up the stairs. I watched her enter my bedroom, where she pulled off her boots and crawled barefoot into my bed. She pulled the covers up to her chin and rolled over to her side. Deep, steady breathing followed quickly.

I sat on the bedroom floor, leaning my back against the wall. Why had she come? Or perhaps, I had come to her, a shadowy figure conjured up in fever dreams, first trying to snatch her from under the bed. Then in the next dream, I dished out ice cream before dissipating like steam. I watched her sleep peacefully for a while. I was getting sleepy too. I closed my eyes. "Who are you really and why have you come?" I yawned. She stirred in her sleep. "You can hear me now?" She mumbled something I couldn't make out. "What?"

"Go home," she murmured.

I opened my eyes. Had I dozed off? It was still nighttime. "Missy?" I called into the darkness. No response. I staggered to my feet. The bed covers had been pulled back. The bed was empty. I checked under the bed; nothing. The closet was wide open and empty too. I made my way down the hall, checking Kiel's room and then my parents'. All the bedroom closet doors and the hall linen closet were open. In the bathroom, the cabinet doors under the sink were open as well. I combed through the rest of the house, remembering to check the narrow space behind the furnace. Missy was gone. Was she searching for another hiding place or looking for a way out? She said to go home, but how and where? Would she leave me behind just like everyone else? Wait, what if she was looking for the portal, just like I was? If she found it, I would too. It was just a matter of time, something I had plenty of.

* * *

It was near dawn when I returned to the kitchen. I had not found Missy. I had not found the portal. I ran through Eve's comics again in my head. I reasoned that the portal would have to be something that knitted my past, present, and future together, a bridge. She thought the portal was down at the creek. Eve wouldn't have known that the creek was drained for a strip mall. And it couldn't have been the swirling blue hole at the bottom of the pool. The pool was sold the summer we moved in 1966. That hole was probably just a fissure left over from my entrance into this world and not meant to be an exit. The portal was somewhere else.

I carried a cup of coffee out to the front steps. The ceramic mug looked huge in my small hands. A brilliant sunrise began to brighten the sky. Yesterday's fog was gone; it would be a glorious summer day, although a solitary one. I listened hopefully for JP's bike to rattle up the street or for a plane to pass overhead, something, any proof of life. I would even bargain for bickering birds or bees buzzing in the rose bushes beside the front steps.

Finally, I did hear something. I put my coffee cup down on the step and stood up. A tap, tap, tap was coming from inside the closed garage. Although

I had searched the entire house, I had not gone into the garage. I turned the metal handle on the garage door and raised it quickly, letting it bang to a thunderous stop.

I shrieked. There lying on the garage floor just inside the doorway was Missy. Her eyes were closed and she was ghastly white. Her cotton pajamas were filthy. Her hair was different too. Gone was the frizz from the Toni home permanent. I slowly reached out, touched her arm, and then drew my hand back quickly in fear. Her skin had the suppleness of a child but was very cold. I brushed her smooth red hair away from her forehead. There was no thin white scar beside her right eye from when I collided with my mother and a storm window on the stairs. I checked Missy's left ring finger. No scar from when the kitchen screen door almost severed my finger at age 3. It seemed as though this replica no longer carried the proof of my childhood. She couldn't be me. Then who was she? "Missy, Missy, what happened?" I screeched, gently shaking her. There was no response. I lifted her limp torso off the ground and cradled her in my lap. The hammer she must have used to tap on the garage door slid out of her hand. Without opening her eyes, she stirred slightly. Then with much effort, she raised her arm a few inches and pointed to the back of the garage. Recessed in the darkness along the cement wall was my father's old wooden workbench. The middle cabinet door was ajar a couple of inches. Inside, a blue reflection danced along the back of the workbench, barely visible behind the door. "What are you pointing at?" But I knew. My mouth went dry. "Is it in there?" I whispered.

Missy nodded.

A surge of adrenalin blasted through me, yet I was too stunned to move. I had walked past this massive hulk on my way to the rec room almost daily. Why had I not thought to search it? The workbench had moved with us to Massachusetts and then to my home in New Hampshire. Like an ancient relic, it had survived the passage of time. Missy stirred which made me flinch. She opened her eyes a slit. "Go," she rasped.

My hands began to tremble. "Are you coming with me?" I squeaked.

"I can't. Go."

"I can't just leave you here."

There was a loud rumble. It came from the back of the garage. I twisted around to look; the workbench cabinet doors had flapped open. Swirling against the cabinet's back wall was the watery blue hole, the portal. This hole seemed swifter and much larger than the one at the bottom of the pool. "Missy, what's happening?"

Her eyes fluttered and then closed. A tremor rocked her, and then she began to wither like a dying flower. The swirling blue hole gained momentum as if scavenging energy from Missy. Then her body became translucent like an embryo. "No!" I cradled her weightless body until she faded completely, mesmerized by the metamorphosis that my mind could not grasp. Missy drew from her life force, and it had cost her. And now I had to leap through a swiftly-moving hole that would probably thrash me against the walls of the workbench before I could slip through. I was terrified. I could still make a life here, couldn't I? Maybe my family would return. Yet, if I didn't go now, I'd be stuck here forever, and Missy's sacrifice would have been for nothing. The churning, blue hole began to slow; I looked out the garage door at my beautiful world one last time. Sucking in a long breath, I grabbed the edge of a cabinet door in each hand and hurled myself headfirst into the swirling blue hole.

The whirlpool slowed as it wrapped gently around me. The water was surprisingly warm and soothing like a hot tub. The terror I had felt dissipated. Then the whirlpool came to a stop as if to allow me to disembark from its merry-go-round. I slid out and was immediately plunged into an underwater tunnel of vibrant blues and greens. I remembered this place. I drifted along on a gentle current, untethered like a dinghy loose from its mooring. I prayed it would ferry me back home safely and not to my death.

* * *

Muffled beeping sounds echoed off the tunnel's walls. Above me was a globe of light. I spread my arms and legs and swam upward toward the light and to wherever I was supposed to go.

As I neared the surface, I bumped against a transparent hard layer like that on a frozen pond. Above this glassy layer, fuzzy shadow heads stared down at me. They all spoke at once, but I could not decipher their insistent, muffled words. I pressed my ear against the layer. One shadow head with a male voice kept shouting one word, something like bead or read, then more slowly, he said, *breathe*. He wanted me to breathe? How strange. I've been breathing all along, hadn't I? He seemed insistent. I drew in a long slow breath. Immediately there was a searing pain in my throat. When I exhaled, a spidery crack spread across the surface of the glass-like layer.

The voice, coming in much clearer now, said, "That's it. Now take another breath. Come on, Honey."

I did. Then the layer broke away completely. I was surrounded by a light so blinding that I had to squeeze my eyes shut. Someone kissed my cheek. There was a familiar scent of aftershave. Squinting, I reached up to touch the blurry face, but something was in the way. On my index finger, I could make out a small plastic clamp. The rest of my hand was attached to a narrow board and wrapped in gauze. I was in a hospital.

"Hey, Babe."

"John?" I said in a hoarse voice I did not recognize.

"Yep. Welcome back."

I opened my eyes a little wider, letting the hospital room come into focus. A ring of people wearing lab coats crowded around my bed.

"Renee, how do you feel?" a woman nearest me asked.

I could not answer. My mind was a soupy grog of anger, fear, and loss. A nurse in scrubs and a ginger beard raised the head of my bed. He smiled at me while he took my blood pressure. The woman continued, "My name is Dr. Lynn Yesko. I'm a pathologist here at Beth Israel Deaconess Medical Center."

"I feel kind of strange and my throat hurts," I rasped, raising my untethered hand to my throat. There was a bandage taped under my ear. "Why am I here?"

Dr. Yesko moved closer to the bed. "We just removed your breathing tube. Try not to talk too much," she said. Two men in lab coats shifted nervously from one foot to another. Then they all looked expectantly at Dr. Yesko. "Renee, you contracted Encephalitis." She let that sink in before continuing. "The bacteria spread very quickly through your lymph nodes. Unfortunately, your body wasn't responding well to the usual antibiotics we tried, so we had to put you into a medically induced coma and intubate you. And then a lymph node under your ear formed a cyst."

"Things were touch and go," interjected John. "You had a couple of seizures, and then." John's eyes welled up. "Your heart stopped."

The cloudiness in my head began to dissipate. "I went somewhere, John," I wheezed.

There was an uncomfortable silence in the room. Dr. Yesko fiddled with the stethoscope around her neck, then gestured to the circle of white coats. "These are my students. Since you weren't responding well to the antibiotics, we did a spinal tap to figure out why. We also biopsied the cyst on your lymph node. What we found was very odd. At first, we thought the lab had mixed up patients because the cyst biopsy and the spinal tap fluid appeared to have come from two separate people. When we redid the tests and examined the results further, we discovered that the cyst carried a second set of DNA."

Nausea began to work its way up my throat. "John, I think I'm gonna be sick," I said, rolling over on my side.

John whirled around, grabbed a Styrofoam cup from the bedside table, and stuck it under my chin just as I began to dry heave. "Can you give her a minute?" he said with a bit of an edge.

"Sure, sure. I can come back later. This is a lot for her to take in right now," Dr. Yesko said, backing out of the room.

"No, no; I want to hear more," I wheezed, flopping back on the bed. "Just let me catch my breath." The smiling, bearded nurse pushed through the crowd of doctors and retook my vital signs. He gave me a wink as he pulled off the blood pressure cuff. "So, how is it possible to carry two sets of DNA, Dr. Yesko?" I asked.

"It's very rare. There are only about thirty documented cases in the world. You're what we call a Chimera. Your blood and all of your organs carry the same DNA, but in that cyst, we found the second set of DNA."

Her words ping-ponged around in my head, popping like bubbles before I could grasp them. I opened my mouth to speak, but a coughing fit silenced me.

Dr. Yesko cleared her throat. "You need to rest. We'll talk more later, I promise."

* * *

After the band of doctors left, John sat on the bed. I sipped apple juice through a straw from a Styrofoam cup he held for me. I told him that I went to Heaven and it was Colonia and that I was 11 again. I could tell by his forced smile that he didn't believe me. Who would?

"You've been through a lot, Renee." He got off the bed and went to the window. "You should see what's going on outside. You've got your CNN, your MSNBC, and the Associated Press. They're all camped out in the parking lot. Oh, and Mr. Good Morning himself, George Stephanopoulos, called. He wants to interview you when you're feeling up to it."

"All this for me?"

John came back to the bed and fluffed up my pillow. "You're a miracle of Nature, Babe."

When Dr. Yesko returned that evening, John was trying to force-feed me lime Jell-O. "Feeling a little bit better?" she asked, unwinding the stethoscope around her neck.

"Still a bit fuzzy. What did you say I was again? Sounded like chimichanga or something."

She smiled as she listened to my heart. "Chimera. In Greek mythology, it refers to a monster that is part goat, part lion, and part snake."

"Jesus, that sounds awful."

"I know. However, in human biology, a Chimera is an organism with at least two genetically distinct types of cells. In your case, it happened at conception. Two fertilized eggs with distinct sets of DNA were supposed to become twins. Instead, the eggs fused, becoming one embryo. As the embryo grew, the dominant twin, which was you, incorporated the cells of the other, bringing along the second set of DNA."

My heart clubbed my chest. "So what you're saying is that I ate my twin?"

Dr. Yesko chuckled. "No, No. Your twin never actually existed, just a few strands of her DNA, which existed only microscopically. We found the DNA strands in that one lymph node, mostly in the cyst. We removed the cyst along with the lymph node." She pointed to the bandage on my neck. "You no longer carry the second set of DNA, but we saved the tissue. There are lots of scientists who want to study it."

A wave of dizziness made me list to one side. John caught me. The twin was a she. Then it was true; the she was Missy. And she had sacrificed herself, an offering to the universe to save me. "I met her, my twin I mean. Her name was Missy."

Dr. Yesko wrinkled her forehead. She gave me a sympathetic smile. "Encephalitis causes swelling of the brain. Hallucinations and strange dreams are very common. You need your rest."

After John fell asleep with his feet outstretched on the vinyl easy chair, I flipped through the TV channels. All the cable outlets were covering me. They showed my high school yearbook photo, a wedding photo, and a School 17 class picture. The CNN headline crawler read *Modern-day Chimera emerges from coma.* MSNBC aired an interview with Dr. Yesko, then did a segment on Greek mythology and the mythical Chimera.

A woman poked her head in the door. "HELLO THERE."

"Audrey!"

When she swooped down to give me a big hug, I stole a glance down her gaping V-neck t-shirt. A ropey scar nestled between her breasts. That disturbing cloudiness in my head returned.

"HOW YA FEELING, MISS CHIMERA?"

"Oh, so you've heard."

"WHAT? HANG ON. LEMME RAISE THE VOLUME ON MY HEARING AID." Audrey pressed something inside one ear. "Yeah, John filled us in."

"I'm still a bit hazy. This is all so crazy. I need to ask you something, though."

"Shoot."

"How's your heart, Audrey?" I stammered.

"What a funny thing to bring up. You mean my heart defect? I'm fine, Renee. It was fixed back in the 60s. Remember?"

"It was my fault, wasn't it, Audrey?"

She laughed. "It was nobody's fault. Jumping rope that day in the yard saved me. If I hadn't gone to the hospital, who knows how long it would've taken to detect the birth defect. I was a ticking time bomb."

I just stared at her, numb but relieved. I had not almost killed my sister.

Encephalitis had indeed ravished my brain, but my psyche had taken me to a place of safety and wonderment, at least for a while. It was still a gift, not just for me but for Missy too. And with searing clarity, I realized that the force field was not meant for me; it was meant for Missy to keep her contained so she wouldn't swallow up the twin that was meant to live. Missy realized this too. She knew we had to part, and this time it would be forever. So Missy searched for the portal to take me home. And when she found it, she helped me through it, knowing she could never follow.

EPILOGUE

By the time I was released from the hospital, the late summer leaves had begun to scatter across the lawn, and John had stretched the winter cover over the pool. Although he never closed the pool this early, he probably figured I wasn't ready to face the place where I had almost drowned.

We pretended to ignore the cable news vans blocking the cul-de-sac and the nosy neighbors strolling nonchalantly past our house. I never did an interview with George Stephanopoulos. The gawkers in front of my house were intrusive enough.

One morning, over a couple of cups of coffee, John told me the full story of what had happened that summer morning. From the bathroom window, he had watched me dive off the diving board, pop up, climb out of the pool, and then back to the diving board. He said when he stepped onto the deck to tell me he was leaving for work, he saw our neighbor, Dan, run across the backyard toward the pool, yelling that I was drowning. They both dragged me out of the pool, unconscious but breathing. By the time the ambulance arrived, I had suffered a couple of seizures. Although Dan probably watched me through his game camera, I was grateful that he found me. Sadly, I was never able to thank Dan. He died suddenly of a heart attack the day after rescuing me. I wondered if the shock of my near drowning and the exertion of helping John pull me out of the water had caused his heart attack.

Months later, my mind was still a conflicted mess. I couldn't be sure if I recalled real childhood memories or Encephalitis fever dreams. The confusion got worse concerning the items I had squirreled away in the Pack-A-Way Self Storage unit. Several times I had visited the unit, picking up treasures that had always held precious childhood memories, but now these treasures betrayed those memories. The children's cookbook with the grease stain on the peanut butter cookie page no longer reminded me of rushing home after Brownies to make them. Instead, I pictured myself trapped alone in the kitchen with a pan full of cookies and no one to share them with. The old *TV Guides* I had collected over the years reminded me of the continuous looping of *Let's Make a Deal* down in the rec room. So I emptied the storage unit and donated or sold everything.

* * *

When winter closed us in, I replied to a few of the hundreds of e-mails from well-wishers (only the ones who weren't looking for money or to bless their cat). There was one e-mail that made me gasp with excitement. It had come in while I was in the hospital. It was from an Edlawn12, and the subject line read, Eve from Colonia. I cupped my hand over my mouth as I read Eve's short message:

Hi Renee,

You probably don't remember me, but I lived across the street from you in Colonia. Just wanted to drop you a line to wish you well. If you're ever in Colonia, I'd love to see you.

I read and reread Eve's e-mail several times. The signature lines said she was a realtor. There was also a photo of a woman freeze-framed at about 40 years old. I didn't recognize the face.

Dr. Yesko was presenting my case at a medical convention in NYC and wanted me to attend. I could swing down to New Jersey after the convention and see Eve, but I couldn't shake the feeling that if I went back to Colonia, I'd be trapped there again. It was silly, I told myself. Then I wrote Eve back and said I would be in town.

She simply replied, "Groovy."

We met at the School 17 parking lot, now a daycare center. I pulled up next to Eve's shiny white Cadillac Escalade. Eve's chestnut hair was now a stylish light brown with salon-curated blonde highlights crowning her head. We leaned into each other, our thick midsections Eskimo kissed as we hugged. We made awkward small talk while we assessed each other's aging features.

Eve linked her arm in mine. "Let's take a stroll down Memory Lane."

A flush of heat spread across my brow. "Umm. Can we get a cup of coffee first?"

Eve unlinked her arm and studied me. "You look like you could use something stronger."

Dr. Yesko warned me to avoid alcohol, but I figured one drink couldn't hurt. Eve pointed a key fob at her car. The Cadillac's doors unlocked with an alert squawk.

We sat in a darkened tavern on Inman Avenue. I nursed a glass of white wine while Eve sipped a Bloody Mary through a fat straw. I had already made up my mind that I wasn't going to say anything about Missy or about traveling back in time. "So whatever happened to the neighborhood kids?" I asked instead.

"Albert is a Navy chaplain. And Paddy McGill, he goes by Pat now, is a cop right here in Colonia. Sometimes he shows up at my open houses."

I took a generous gulp of wine, then another, letting the tension ebb from my body. My heart calmed. "I can picture Pat a cop." And what about JP?" I blurted before I realized that I did. Geez.

I held my breath while Eve swirled a stalk of celery in her glass. "JP didn't make it. Died in an automobile accident."

My stomach crinkled. I took another sip of wine. "You know I wanted to warn JP about wearing seatbelts."

Eve cocked her head. "You did? When was that? Didn't you move like in 1966?"

Why had I said that? To absolve me of the guilt I felt? Maybe I could have saved him. Or maybe it was his or Audrey's life that could be saved, but not both. I'll never know. Eve was staring at me, waiting for an answer. "Umm. Yeah, you're right. I still have false memories. I must have dreamt it," I stammered. "So how about you, Eve? How did you fare growing up?"

Eve ditched her straw and took a long gulp from her Bloody Mary. "I did alright. The real estate business is booming. My old house came on the market about five years ago, and I sold it!" she beamed.

The waitress came over, and we ordered another round. I shooed away Dr. Yesko's warning.

"So wait. How long were you living at home, Eve? The last time I saw you was at our barbecue. You took off when you overheard my mother talk about your mother."

"Yeah, I know," Eve said, bowing her head. "I guess I was embarrassed."

"But where'd you go, Eve? Did your father whisk you off to a work farm in Pennsylvania?" I wasn't sure if I had actually said those words out loud or not. My mouth felt detached from my brain. The waitress walked by with a tray of dirty glasses. I asked her for a glass of ice water.

Eve gave me a strange, confused look. "Nooo. Who told you that? I ran away."

"You did?"

"Yeah, but not far. Just to my aunt's house. I got into a big fight with my father over what your mother said. I stormed out of the house and called my aunt from the phone booth at Lake's."

"What did he tell you about your mother?"

"Oh, it was so long ago, Renee. All I remember is that he was mad that I had questioned him."

"But why didn't you let me know where you were? I was worried."

"I know. I know. I guess I felt ashamed."

"How long were you gone?"

Eve didn't speak for a long time. She stabbed at a wedge of lime at the bottom of her glass with the stalk of celery. "It was just supposed to be for a couple of days. But then my father...he killed himself, Renee. Jumped off the Inman Avenue overpass."

"What? Oh my God, Eve! I'm so sorry."

"Yeah. You had already moved. I guess he was pretty drunk. After that, I just stayed with my aunt until I graduated from high school. I was all messed up, Renee. I knew he was mean, but the poor guy. First, my mother leaves him and then me. I guess he just couldn't take it. I blamed myself."

I reached across the table and held her hand. "Eve, it's not your fault. You were just a kid."

"That's what everyone kept telling me."

"Eve, listen to me. Are you really sure your mother ran off? I mean, have you done any searches online? You know, searched by her Social Security number?"

Eve's eyes narrowed. She gently slid her hand out of mine. "I think you should lay off the wine, Renee. You're talking crazy now."

"So I guess that means you haven't done any searches. What if your mother never left?"

"What do you mean?" she said with an edge of irritation.

"What I mean is, what if she wanted to leave with you, but he wouldn't let her."

Eve smoothed out her cocktail napkin and then folded it into neat quarters.

I lowered my head and whispered, "What if he killed her."

Eve slapped her palms on the table. "Renee quit it. You don't know what you're talking about. Your brain's fried. I get it. But to go around accusing people of murder." She signaled to the waitress for the check.

* * *

I called Eve that evening, but she wouldn't pick up. I left a voice mail telling her I was sorry for upsetting her. Later that night, my phone buzzed with a New Jersey number I didn't recognize. I was surprised to hear Paddy's voice on the other end. He wanted to know if my parents were still alive. If they were, he wanted to interview them. Although Eve was pissed at me, what I said must have bugged her enough to call Paddy. Perhaps she would call me back. It pained me to know that our rekindled friendship had ended like that.

"They're both deceased, Paddy. I mean Pat. But I can tell you that my mother never believed Mr. Caruso's story. Did you do a records search?"

"Eve did. She called me. There's no trace of her after 1960. I checked a couple of law enforcement databases too, but there's nothing. She still could have left, changed her name. Many women did back then, and it was easier to disappear."

"If she's still alive, Pat, why hasn't she tried to contact Eve?"

He let out a long breath. "I don't know."

The next morning, I checked out of the hotel. I tried Eve's number again. It went straight to voice mail.

* * *

Five years went by without a word from Eve. We sold the house along with the workbench and moved to Florida. I was still in bed on an early spring morning when my cell phone rang. It was Eve. "We found my mother," she said gravely.

I sat up in bed. "Eve! That's great. Where?"

Her voice was barely audible. "Under the patio."

"No!"

Eve said the homeowners were digging a foundation for an addition when the excavator dug up a heap of women's clothes. Underneath the clothes wrapped in a stained bedspread was a human skeleton. "They're doing DNA testing, but I know it's her, Renee. I recognized the dress from an old photo."

We talked for a long time. Later that month, Eve e-mailed me links to newspaper articles about the case. The DNA tests confirmed that the remains were that of Juanita Caruso. And although not conclusive, the police believed that Mr. Caruso killed her. Eve said that a heavy weight had been lifted off her chest. She wasn't the cause of her father's suicide, and her mother hadn't abandoned her.

Eve and I speak often now. I finally told her about Missy, describing us as two branches from the same tree. And that I still feel her in my soul. And Eve believes me.

About the Author

Denise Sawyer

Denise Sawyer was born in Colonia, New Jersey, squished in the middle of an older brother and two younger sisters. During the lazy days of summer, Denise wrote skits—mainly tragedies, which were performed by the neighborhood kids in garages and backyards.

Her debut on the publishing scene, showcasing her signature folksy style, came in early 2016 with her humorous essay told through her mother's voice called "Making Manicotti" published in the literary journal *Dead Housekeeping*.

Other published works include her cheeky poem about wild turkeys eating everything in her yard called "Wild Feathered Foes" published in the *Manatee Literary Journal* and her short story inspired by her boisterous Italian relatives called "The Neighbor," published in the *Scarlet Leaf Review*. Denise is currently working on her memoir *Spinning Plates* chronicling her heart-breaking quest to rid her teenage niece of an abusive boyfriend. Through this memoir, Denise hopes to highlight the growing problem of Teen Dating Abuse.

Denise graduated Summa Cum Laude with a B.A. in Creative Writing and English from Southern New Hampshire University and is an active member of the New Hampshire Writers' Project. She lives in New Hampshire where her father's old wooden workbench still resides in the garage.

Author's Note

The inspiration for *A Swim Back Home*, a story that has lived within me my entire life, came from my own childhood experience of moving from Colonia, New Jersey to Massachusetts at the age of 11. Many of the scenes — such as the pool collapse, Audrey's heart condition, and JP's cigarette racket are based on actual events. I have done my best to accurately portray Lake's candy store, School 17, and the homes and streets as they appeared in 1966.

Although *A Swim Back Home* is a work of fiction, the Chimera phenomenon is science fact. Renee's condition is loosely based on the modern-day Chimera, Karen Keegan. Her case is documented in *The New England Journal of Medicine* which can be found here: https://www.nejm.org/doi/full/10.1056/NEJMoa013452

Lastly, the characters in the novel are a somewhat twisted version of my childhood friends and family. Thank you Allison, Nanette, Neil, Pat, Arthur, Jeff, Jean Pierre, Uncle Gene, Anne, Melinda, and John Patrick!

References

Yu, Neng, et al. "Disputed Maternity Leading to Identification of Tetragametic Chimerism." *New England Journal of Medicine*, vol. 346, no. 20, 2002, pp. 1545–1552., https://www.nejm.org/doi/full/10.1056/NEJMoa013452.

"She's Her Own Twin." *ABC News*, ABC News Network, 15 Aug. 2015, https://abcnews.go.com/.

1960's References

TV Shows mentioned:

- *The Patty Duke Show* (TV show, 1963-1966)

- *Let's Make a Deal* (game show, begun in 1963)

- *Lost in Space* (TV show, 1965-1968)

- *The Man from U.N.C.L.E.* (TV show, 1964-1968 - leading characters were Illya Kuryakin, played by David McCallum, and Napoleon Solo, played by Robert Vaughn)

- *I Dream of Jeannie* (TV show, 1965-1970)

- *The Twilight Zone* (TV show, 1959-1964)

- *Dr. Kildare* (TV show, 1961-1966)

- *The Edge of Night* (afternoon soap opera, 1956-1984)

- *Looney Tunes* (animated comedy short film series that spawned multiple cartoon TV shows, films and comic books, beginning in 1930)

Books, Magazines mentioned:

- *Journey into Mystery* series (comic book series beginning in the 1950s)

- *Marvel Comics* series (comic book series beginning in 1961)

- *Fantastic Four* (comic book series beginning in 1961)

- *Strange Tales* (Marvel Comics anthology series. 1951 - 1968)

- ***Highlights for Children*** (American children's magazine began publication in June, 1946)

- ***The Evergreen Review*** (literary magazine from 1961 - 1984)

- ***TV Guide*** (weekly listings of TV shows, first issue was in 1953)

- ***Playboy*** (monthly men's magazine, first issue was in 1953)

Games mentioned:

- ***Candyland*** (Hasbro board game originally published in 1949)

- ***Chutes and Ladders*** (made by Milton Bradley Company beginning in 1943)

Toys mentioned:

- ***Colorforms*** (creative toy of simple shapes and forms cut from colored vinyl sheeting that cling to a smooth backing surface without adhesives; manufactured by Colorforms Brand, LLC, and available from 1951 to present)

- ***Magic 8-Ball*** (fortune-telling toy originally invented in 1946; currently manufactured by Mattel)

- ***View-Master*** (Sterorscope viewer with special "reel" of 3-D photographs, by Mattel in 1962)

- ***Schwinn Wasp*** bicycle (made from 1954 - 1964)

Popular cars of the 1960s mentioned:

- *Mustang* *convertible* (made by Ford Motors beginning in 1964)

- *Rambler* *station wagon* (made by American Motors 1955 - 1969)

Popular beer brands mentioned:

- *Schlitz* (first produced by Joseph Schlitz Brewing Company in 1849)

Popular cigarette brands mentioned:

- *Kools* (introduced in 1933)

- *Salems* (introduced in 1956)

- *Winston Menthols* (introduced in 1954)

- *Pall Malls* (introduced in 1899)

For more information about these and other brands, see Wikipedia at https://en.wikipedia.org/wiki/Main_Page

www.ingramcontent.com/pod-product-compliance
Lightning Source LLC
Chambersburg PA
CBHW030802190726
48285CB00003B/977